ADDY

1864

FINDING FREEDOM

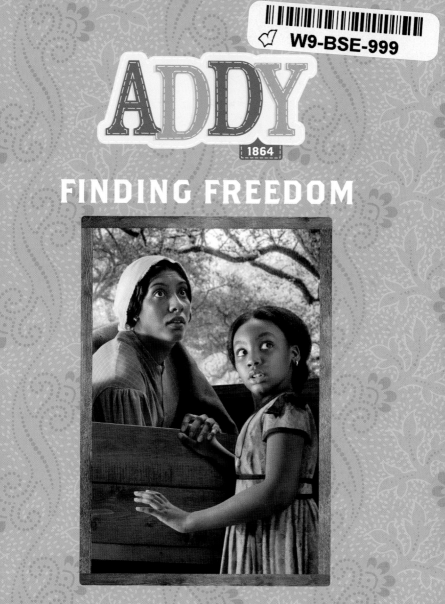

BY CONNIE PORTER

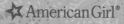
American Girl®

A PEEK INTO
ADDY'S
WORLD

Addy and her family are enslaved on a plantation in North Carolina. The tiny cabin is the only home Addy has ever known, and she's never been farther than the edge of the plantation.

1. SLAVE QUARTERS

2. BARN

3. OVERSEER'S HOUSE

4. BIG HOUSE

5. KITCHEN

--- ADDY'S FAMILY & FRIENDS ---

MOMMA
Addy's mother

POPPA
Addy's father

SAM
Addy's fifteen-year-old brother

ESTHER
Addy's one-year-old sister

AUNTIE LULA
The cook on the plantation,
who is like family to Addy

UNCLE SOLOMON
Auntie Lula's husband

MISS CAROLINE
A woman who helps Momma and Addy

MISS DUNN
Addy's teacher

SARAH
Addy's friend

MRS. MOORE
Sarah's mother

HARRIET
Addy's classmate

MRS. FORD
The owner of the dress shop where Momma works

Addy's story is written in a dialect that reflects the way African Americans spoke in Addy's time. The dialect isn't written exactly the way people spoke. That would make the book too difficult to read. Instead, the dialect is similar to how speech sounded at the time.

TABLE OF CONTENTS

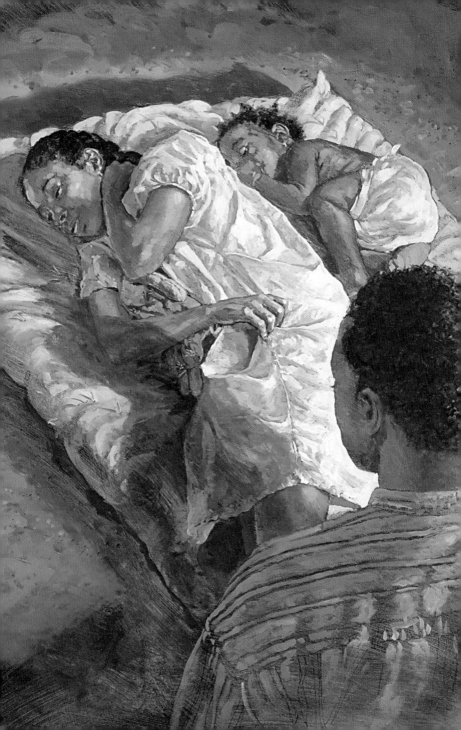

WHISPERS OF FREEDOM
∾ Chapter 1 ∾

Addy Walker woke up late on a summer's night to hear her parents whispering. She liked the sound. It made her feel safe, knowing her mother and father were close by.

A small fire glowed in the hearth. It was the only light in the windowless cabin, but tonight it made her hot and uncomfortable. The stiff, dry cornhusks stuffing her pallet poked through their thin covering, sticking her. Addy's older brother, Sam, lay on his own pallet near her feet, and her baby sister, Esther, lay next to her. Esther's steamy breath was blowing on Addy's face. Addy loved Esther, but it was too hot to be close to her tonight. Addy tried to wiggle away from the baby. When she turned from Esther, her parents stopped talking.

"Hush, Ben," Momma said to Poppa. "I think Addy woke up."

Addy kept her eyes closed, but she could hear the rustle of cornhusks when her father got up. His feet softly crossed the dirt floor.

"That child asleep, Ruth," Poppa said to Momma,

returning to their pallet. "She tired out. They had the children out in the fields half the day worming the tobacco plants."

"Ben, listen to me," Momma said. Her voice was serious. "I don't think we should run now. The war is gonna be over soon, and then we'll be free."

"Ruth, I've done told you before, them Union soldiers ain't nowhere near our part of North Carolina. They all the way clear on the other side of the state," Addy's father replied. "Who knows when we gonna be free?"

"But Ben, we can't lose nothing by waiting. We all together here. That count for something," Momma argued.

"It should count, but you know it don't. With this war, times hard. Money is real tight for the masters. A whole group of slaves was sold off the Gifford plantation because Master Gifford couldn't afford to feed them," Poppa said.

"That was Master Gifford. Master Stevens would never sell us. We work hard for him. He need me to do sewing, and you do his carpenter work." Addy had never heard her mother speak so firmly.

"What about Sam?" Poppa went on. "I got to drag him off his pallet when the morning work horn sound. He get up grumbling about not wanting to work for the master, and he take his grumbling out into the fields. Sam done run off once, and now he want to go fight in the war. If

Sam don't watch it, he gonna be getting us all in trouble."

Addy didn't like what she heard. She remembered when Sam had run off the year before, shortly before Esther was born. He was tracked down by Master Stevens's dogs and brought back. Sam was tied to a tree, and Master Stevens beat him with a whip. Addy screamed and cried, but her parents did not. They had blank, empty faces that made Addy angry. When the beating was over, Poppa carried Sam back to the cabin, and Momma cleaned the blood from Sam's back. None of them said a word. Finally, Addy yelled at her parents, "Y'all don't care about Sam at all! Y'all not even crying." As soon as she said it, she felt bad.

"Just because you don't see us crying and carrying on don't mean we don't care," Poppa had said softly. "It don't mean we ain't crying, either. Me and your momma crying on the inside. We ain't always free to show our feelings on the outside. But on the inside we is free. There's always freedom inside your head, Addy."

Freedom. That was what her parents were talking about tonight. But they were talking about a different kind of freedom. They were talking about the kind of freedom a slave had to run away to get.

"If Sam take off by himself a second time, we might never see him again," Momma said in a worried whisper. "I want us all to be together."

Poppa didn't answer right away. Then he said, "Uncle Solomon told me that there's a set of railroad tracks about ten miles after the river near the Gifford place. We follow them north till they cross another set of tracks. Where they cross, there's a white house with red shutters. It's a safe house. A white woman live there, named Miss Caroline. She gonna help us. We only got to get that far," Poppa said.

In the dark, Addy hugged Janie, the small rag doll Momma had made for her, the doll she slept with every night. Her parents' talk about running away scared her. She had never heard them talk about it before. Whenever Sam talked about escaping, they told him to hush up.

"If we get caught, Master Stevens gonna split us up for sure," Momma said, her voice shaky.

"Ain't nothing for sure," answered Poppa, "but we got to take our chances while we got 'em. You can't go backing out on me now."

"I'm not backing out," Momma said. "I'm just scared. You want to go all the way to Philadelphia. I ain't never been no farther than the Gifford plantation. What if we get lost from each other?"

"We gonna go together, and we gonna stay together. God will watch over us. You got to believe we gonna make it north, Ruth." Poppa sounded sure and strong. Addy knew he could protect them, no matter what.

"Let's just wait a little longer. When the war over, we all gonna be free. All of us right here," Momma said again.

But Poppa was firm. "I hurt when I see Addy toting heavy water buckets to the fields, or when I see her working there, bent over like a old woman. Sam already fifteen, but she a little girl, nine years old, and smart as they come. She go out in the morning, her eyes all bright and shining with hope. By night she come stumbling in here so tired, she can hardly eat. She getting beat down every day. I can't stand back and watch it no more. We can't wait for our freedom. We gonna have to take it."

Addy waited for her mother's answer, but none came. She heard her father rise. He went to the hearth and covered the coals with ashes.

When Addy heard him lie down, her eyes popped open, but she couldn't see anything. In the thick darkness, Addy knew she had heard a secret that she must keep to herself no matter how hot it burned inside her. She could feel Esther's breath on her back. Turning to face her sister, Addy moved close and put her arms around her. The baby's breath did not feel too warm now. Addy was glad Esther was there with her.

SOLD!
⌇ Chapter 2 ⌇

arly the next morning, Addy was in the tobacco field worming the plants. She and the other children moved from row to row, carefully pulling green, wiggling worms from the leaves. The worms were as fat as her fingers, but Addy tried not to think about them. Instead, she dreamed about the kind of freedom Momma and Poppa had talked about the night before—the kind slaves ran away for. She imagined herself learning to read and write and wearing fancy dresses that Momma would make for her.

By eleven o'clock the sun was high overhead, and Addy felt as if she'd worked all day. She had just finished worming her rows when it was time for her next chore, taking water to the field hands. The full bucket of water she carried was heavy. As Addy struggled with the bucket, sweat ran down her dark face and soaked the neck of her rough cotton shift. But she liked this chore because she sometimes had a chance to see Sam or Poppa. On this day, she saw Sam. As usual, he had a riddle for her.

"Riddle me this," said Sam. "What's smaller than a

dog but can put a bear on the run?"

Addy thought hard as Sam took the dipper from the bucket and poured some water over his head.

From a few rows away the overseer snarled, "That water's for drinkin', boy."

Addy saw a scowl come over Sam's face. He mumbled, "Even a horse got to stop and cool off sometime."

"I better get on," Addy said, worried that the overseer might come over to them. He carried a whip.

"Naw," Sam said, his face softening. He was as tall as Poppa, but he was skinny. When he smiled, Sam still looked like a little boy. "I ain't done drinking yet, and you ain't answered my riddle. What's smaller than a dog but can put a bear on the run?" he repeated.

He took a drink while Addy looked to see where the overseer was. He had gone off in another direction. Addy crinkled up her eyebrows and said, "A skunk?"

"You right! You too smart, girl. Pretty soon you gonna be riddling me," Sam said.

Addy paused for a moment. She wanted to tell Sam what she had heard their parents talking about the night before. But the escape plan was so dangerous that she could not share it with anyone. She had to keep the secret inside.

"See you later," Addy said to Sam before moving down the row to give the next field hand a drink. When the bucket was empty, she headed toward the kitchen to help Auntie Lula serve dinner to Master Stevens.

::

The kitchen was a small brick building behind the big house. Auntie Lula was ready for Addy to work as soon as Addy stepped into the building. "Wash your hands good," Auntie Lula said, "and take that tray of food and water to the dining room."

"Yes, ma'am," Addy answered. She liked Auntie Lula, who was old enough to be Addy's grandmother. Auntie Lula's skin was light and her rusty red hair was streaked with gray. She looked after Addy and her family, giving them medicine when they were sick.

The dinner Auntie Lula had cooked for Master Stevens smelled so good that Addy ached for a bite of it. All she had had for breakfast was cornmeal mush, and that was all she would have for dinner. Maybe Auntie Lula would hide away a few scraps for Addy to eat today.

Addy washed and dried her hands and then picked up the tray and hurried to the dining room. Master Stevens was sitting at the table with another white man. She set the food on the table and then poured water for both men. As they began to eat, she went to stand quietly in the corner.

"You got that little girl trained real good," the man said to Master Stevens.

"I got them all trained real good," said Master Stevens. "That's why it's such a shame to let any of them go."

Addy's stomach turned when she heard Master Stevens say those words. *What he mean, let go?* she wondered.

"But I have twenty-two slaves to clothe and feed this winter," Master Stevens went on, "and you know how hard it is with the war. I need the money."

Addy stared at the floor, but she was listening very closely. She let her face go blank and empty.

"This boy you got for me," said the man, "how can I be sure he won't run on me? I know he's run before."

"I taught him a lesson with the whip last time he ran off," Master Stevens answered, "and you'll have his father, too. His father can control him."

They were talking about Sam and Poppa! Master Stevens was going to sell them. Her father had been right. Master Stevens was going to split up their family!

"More water," the strange man said, turning to Addy.

Addy hurried to pour him more water.

"You sure you don't want to sell this one?" the man asked Master Stevens, patting Addy on the head.

Addy's hand shook. She wanted to pull away from his touch, to scream. But the blank look was frozen on her face. She filled the man's glass and started to pour water for Master Stevens.

"She's too young now," Master Stevens replied. "Maybe when she's a little older, I'll let her go, too. By then she might fetch a price as good as her brother."

Addy was listening so hard that she forgot to pay attention to her task and filled Master Stevens's glass too full. Water spilled on the table.

"See, I told you she's too young," Master Stevens said to the man. To Addy, he said sharply, "Girl, go get a rag and clean up this mess!"

Addy was glad to have a reason to run back to the kitchen. She burst through the door. "Auntie Lula," she panted. "That man fixing to take Sam and Poppa with him! Master Stevens gonna sell them!"

Auntie Lula looked worried, but when she spoke, her voice was calm.

"If that be true, we don't have much time," Auntie Lula said. "Listen to me good, now. Take your bucket and run to the well. Fill the bucket and head right to the fields where your brother and father at."

"But I already took water," Addy said.

"Hush up, child," Auntie Lula hissed. "You a smart girl. Act like you think it's time for the afternoon water. Walk right out to Sam and your poppa and tell them what you heard. If that man really coming for them, it's the one chance they got to run. I'll go back to the dining room."

Grabbing her bucket, Addy ran to the well as fast as she could. *Please don't let him take Sam and Poppa. Please, God,* she prayed silently as she ran.

When Addy came to the well, she filled her bucket. She tried to run with it, but the water splashed crazily over the sides. With less than half of it left, she headed toward the fields, walking as fast as she could. Her throat was dry. *Sam! Poppa! Where you at?* she screamed inside. Outside, her eyes desperately searched the huge field.

Addy didn't notice the overseer until he stepped right into her path. "Hey, girl!" he barked at her. "What you think you doing?"

Addy was so startled that she dropped her bucket. "I come to bring the afternoon water," she said.

"It ain't time for their afternoon water, you stupid girl. Get on out of here."

Addy felt frantic, but she said nothing more. She picked up her bucket and ran back to the kitchen. When she got there, she saw her mother with Esther and Auntie Lula.

"Momma—" Addy began.

But her mother cut her off. "Auntie Lula told me."

"Master Stevens and that man headed for the barn," Auntie Lula said. "Maybe they got Sam and your poppa there."

Addy's head jerked up. Maybe she could still warn

Sam and Poppa. Addy raced out the door.

"Addy!" Momma called after her. "Wait!"

But Addy did not stop. She was not thinking, not praying, just running, running, running. When she came to the barn, she saw a wagon. Sam was in it, bound and gagged, shackled hand and foot. Master Stevens and the man from the dining room were standing next to the wagon.

"Sam!" Addy cried out when she reached the wagon. "Oh, please, Master Stevens," Addy begged. "Don't let them take Sam."

"Get out of here, Addy," Master Stevens ordered. He had a whip in his hand.

Then Addy heard a deeper voice.

"Addy, go on now." It was her father's voice. But where was he? She looked down and saw him lying on the ground, his feet being chained by the overseer. Poppa's face was covered with dirt, but it was calm. She ran to him, falling on the ground next to him. "Oh, Poppa. No. No!" She threw her arms around him.

"Everything's gonna be all right, honey. You go on," Poppa said. There were no tears on his face, but Addy knew he was crying inside.

"Get back, girl," Master Stevens barked. Addy heard his whip crack. She felt a lash of fire on her back as if she

had been burned. But still she held on to Poppa.

Master Stevens growled at her. "I told you to get. Now get before I whip you again." He reached for Addy and yanked her away from Poppa.

Addy fell backward into her mother's arms. Momma held Addy close, both of them crying. This time, even Momma couldn't keep the pain hidden inside.

A NEW PLAN
ᥱ⁓ Chapter 3 ⁓ᥱ

I t was late afternoon, nearly a week after Sam and Poppa had been sold. Addy and the other children were worming tobacco plants again. They were to work their way down the long rows, turning over every leaf to find the worms and kill them. It was a job Addy hated. She didn't even like looking at the worms. To kill them, she had to either squish them with her hands or squash them under her bare feet.

Addy's mind was not on her work. All her thoughts were about Poppa and Sam. *I got a riddle for you, Sam,* she thought to herself. *What's heavy as a full pail of water but still empty? Give up? It's my heart.* She peeled the worms off some plants but forgot to look under the leaves of others. When she came to the end of her second row, the overseer came along behind her to check her work.

Addy was just starting the next row when the overseer came storming toward her. He had his whip in one hand. Addy raised her hands to shield her face, thinking he was going to hit her.

But he did not hit her. He dropped the whip, grabbed

Addy's wrists in one of his large hands, and opened his other hand. Addy saw what he held—live worms. Worms that Addy had missed. The overseer forced open her mouth and stuffed the still-twisting and wiggling worms inside.

Addy began choking.

"Eat them!" the overseer growled. "Chew them up—every last one of them. If you don't, I'll get some more."

Addy gagged as the worms' juicy bodies burst in her mouth.

"That'll teach you to mind your work," the overseer snapped. He shoved her away. Addy crumpled to the ground as he turned to leave.

It was dark when Momma and baby Esther came home to the cabin that night. There was no fire in the hearth. Addy lay curled up on her pallet.

"Addy, you awake?" her mother asked, lighting a candle and then placing Esther down on the pallet. But Addy did not even look up.

"Addy?" her mother said in a voice as soft and warm as the glow of the candle. She sat down on the edge of Addy's pallet and touched her head gently.

Addy opened her eyes. They were red. As she told her mother about what the overseer had done to her, she started to cry. Momma lifted Addy's head onto her lap. "Momma, I hate them. I hate white people," Addy sobbed.

"I don't want you to hate nobody," Momma said, stroking Addy's hair.

"Don't you hate them, Momma?" Addy asked.

"No, I don't," Momma answered. "Honey, if you fill your heart with hate, there ain't gonna be no room for love. Your brother and Poppa need us to fill our hearts with love for them, not hate for white people."

"But Momma, that overseer and Master Stevens, they hate us," Addy said bitterly. "Why?"

"Addy, all white people don't hate colored people. Master Stevens was wrong to sell Sam and Poppa and to whip you. But people can do wrong for such a long time, they don't even know it's wrong no more. People can hurt each other and not even care they hurting them. Like that overseer. He a mean man. That's what hate do to people. I don't want you to ever be that kind of person."

Esther began crying. Addy reached over and handed her rag doll to the baby. Esther quieted down.

"Addy, there something I need to talk to you about," Momma said slowly, "something serious. Your poppa and me talked about something before Master Stevens sold him and Sam. Poppa was worried about the war, and times getting hard . . ."

Addy knew what her mother was going to say. Addy hadn't forgotten about the secret she had been keeping. "You and Poppa planned for us all to run away," she said.

"How did you know that?" Momma asked.

"I heard y'all talking one night," Addy answered.

"Then you already know we planned to go north," said Momma. "Well, we still going."

"What about Poppa and Sam?" Addy asked. "Shouldn't we wait for them to come back for us?"

"They ain't coming back here ever again, no matter what," Momma replied. "Poppa's plan was to go to Philadelphia. He told Sam about it. I aim to stick to that plan, and we leaving tomorrow night."

Addy looked into her mother's thin face. There were fine lines of worry around her brown eyes.

"But what if we get caught?" Addy asked, her voice shaking.

"There ain't no choice, honey. I never thought Master Stevens would break up our family after your poppa and me served him our whole life. But I was wrong." Momma shook her head. "I can't keep you safe here no more, Addy. I'm scared that man who bought Sam and your poppa might come back for you. I can't stop him if he do. I ain't gonna sit here and wait for him or anybody to come take you from me."

Esther started to cry again, and Addy patted her gently. Then she said, "Momma, I'm scared, but I want to go to freedom."

Momma went to her pallet and pulled something out from under it. There were two large kerchiefs and some clothes. They were not clothes for a woman and a girl, but for a man and a boy.

"Momma, what we gonna do with these?" asked Addy.

"I'm gonna pack them kerchiefs with some food and a drinking gourd. We wearing the clothes," answered Momma.

"We gonna be disguised?" asked Addy in surprise.

Momma nodded. "Auntie Lula and Uncle Solomon got them for us. When Master Stevens send out his dogs after us, it's gonna be hard for them to track our smell if we got on somebody else's clothes."

"Auntie Lula and Uncle Solomon should come with us, Momma," said Addy. "Poppa say Uncle Solomon know where the safe house is. They should come to freedom, too."

"They too old to come to freedom, Addy. They can't run," Momma said. "They would slow us down."

"Esther can't run neither, and she coming," Addy said.

Momma lowered her head. Addy knew something was

wrong. Her mother would not look at her. Then Addy saw tears on her mother's face.

"Momma, what's the matter?" Addy asked.

In a slow, sad voice, her mother said, "Esther ain't coming with us."

Addy could not believe her ears. She picked up Esther and held her close. "No, Momma," Addy said. "We ain't leaving Esther."

Momma's voice was soft but firm. "Your sister is staying here."

"But why? Poppa said we was all going," Addy insisted.

"Honey, it was different when your poppa and Sam was going with us. They could help carry Esther. Now I got to carry her by myself."

"I could help, Momma. Let me carry her," Addy begged.

"Besides," Momma went on, "Esther might cry any time. Her crying would give us away."

"I could keep her quiet, Momma, I just know I could," Addy said. "I'd let her hold Janie while we was running."

"Addy, Esther can't come," her mother said. "This the hardest thing I ever had to do in my life. I love Esther as much as I love you and Sam, but we can't take her. Auntie Lula and Uncle Solomon is gonna keep her. She just a baby, so Master Stevens ain't gonna sell her. He can't make no money selling a baby."

Addy cradled Esther in her arms, gently rocking her back and forth. The three of them sat quietly for a long time. Then Momma broke the silence. "The war ain't gonna last forever. When it's over, we gonna get Esther back. Our family will be together again. Lay down now," Momma said, blowing out the candle.

"Momma, can we all sleep together tonight?" Addy asked.

"I'd like that," Momma said.

Addy, Momma, and Esther crowded onto Addy's pallet. Esther was sandwiched between Addy and Momma. The baby held tight to Janie.

Addy moved as close to Esther as she could to feel the baby's warm breath on her face. She put her arms around her tiny sister. Addy tried not to cry, but itchy, hot tears were running down her face, and she didn't bother brushing them away. She felt her mother's arms around both her and the baby. Beyond, from the deeper darkness of the woods, Addy heard a single owl hooting in the night.

INTO THE NIGHT
✑ Chapter 4 ✑

he next night, after it was fully dark, with not a streak of orange or red in the sky, Auntie Lula and Uncle Solomon came to Addy's cabin. Addy and her mother were in their disguises, with their kerchiefs packed. Esther was sleeping on Addy's pallet.

Uncle Solomon had two hats with him. One was a straw hat that he gave Addy's mother. The other, a felt hat, he placed on Addy's head.

"Now, there's magic in your hat," Uncle Solomon said to Addy, trying to cheer her up. Addy did not feel like smiling.

"Don't you believe that hat got magic?" Uncle Solomon asked. He snapped his fingers near her left ear. "Why, look what's come out your ear. You must've forgot to wash behind it. Look at this half dime I found there." He handed the coin to Addy.

Addy reached behind her ear. "How'd you do that?" she asked.

"It's magic," Uncle Solomon said. "You hold on to that half dime. You gonna need it where you going. Freedom cost, you hear me? Freedom's got its cost."

"Look here, I got some food for you," Auntie Lula said, handing Addy's mother a small sack.

Addy's mother put the sack into her kerchief. Then she bent down to pick up Esther, who woke and began to fuss.

Addy watched Momma as she hugged the baby hard and kissed her over and over. She searched Momma's face for tears, but there weren't any, not on the outside at least.

Addy kissed Esther, too, and stroked her head. She handed her rag doll to the baby. "You hold on to Janie until I see you again," Addy said. Then her mother gave Esther to Auntie Lula.

"We gonna take good care of Esther," Auntie Lula said.

Uncle Solomon gave Addy and Momma some final advice. "Go fast as you can at night and hide during the day. Every time you see water, go through it. A creek, a river—I don't care if it ain't nothing but a puddle, go through it. That way you won't hardly leave no scent for the dogs to pick up on. And watch out for them Confederate soldiers. They dressed up in gray uniforms. They can be mean as snakes, and if they catch you, they gonna bring you back to slavery."

"God be with you," Auntie Lula said as Addy and her

mother turned to leave the little cabin. Esther began to cry as they slipped out into the damp, warm night and ran into the woods. Addy looked back to catch a final glimpse of her baby sister, but tears blurred her sight.

The full moon shone in the eastern sky, looking like a half dime shining in the bottom of a well. At first, the moonlight shone through the tall pines, filling the forest with a silver light. Addy and her mother ran from shadow to shadow like a deer with her fawn. But as they moved deeper into the woods, only a small glimmer of moonlight made its way through the thick branches of the trees. There were dark, eerie shadows everywhere, and it was hard to see. Momma took Addy's hand as they hurried along, stumbling over vines and stumps hidden by the darkness.

Addy expected to hear the comforting night sounds that she always heard at the cabin, but the deeper they got in the woods, the stranger the sounds became. Owls screeched high in the pines, and the wind moaned like a wounded animal.

Suddenly a dark form stirred in the bushes ahead, moving toward them. Addy screamed and froze. Momma jerked to a stop and clamped her hand over Addy's mouth.

"Hush up," her mother whispered sharply. "You can't holler out."

The bushes moved again. Addy's heart beat very fast. Bump-bump-bump-bump. Bump-bump-bump-bump.

Slowly, Momma took her hand away from Addy's mouth. "It's only a possum or a skunk," she said calmly.

"I ain't mean to holler," Addy whispered. "We left Esther behind because her crying might give us away. But I hollered louder than Esther ever could." Addy remembered what her father had said about not always showing your feelings. She would have to learn to keep them inside sometimes.

All through the night, Addy and Momma stumbled through the darkness. They waded through swampy places where their feet were sucked deep into oozing mud. They clawed through prickly vines. The thorns dug into Addy's hands until they bled. Once she stubbed her toe on a rock and fell down. But this time Addy did not cry out. All night long, she and Momma pushed on and on.

Just when Addy thought she could not go another step, the sky began to lighten. "We better stop soon, Momma," Addy said softly. "It's getting light out and somebody might see us."

Momma nodded. "We need to look for a hiding place."

They went a little farther and found a small cave. They crawled inside and huddled together. Addy fell asleep almost instantly.

When she woke up hours later, it was hot. Mosquitoes buzzed around her head, drawn to the stickiness of her sweaty skin. Addy slapped at them, but it was no use.

"You must be hungry," Momma said, reaching into her bundle. She handed Addy a piece of Auntie Lula's corn bread. It was hard and dry, but it tasted good to Addy. She washed it down with a drink of water from the gourd.

When they finished eating, Momma reached into the bundle again and pulled out a small, shiny shell.

"This is something me and your poppa been saving for you," Momma said. "This cowrie shell belonged to Poppa's grandma. She was stole from Africa when she was no bigger than you. None of her family was on the ship with her when she came here from across the water. She wore this shell on a necklace. Your great-grandma's name was Aduke. That name got a meaning where she come from. It means 'much loved.' I saved her name for you, Addy."

Addy looked into her mother's gentle brown eyes. "Can I hold the shell?"

"Sure you can. I got something special to put it on," her mother said, pulling a leather string out of her bundle.

"That's one of Sam's shoelaces!" Addy said.

"I wanted you to have something of his, too," Momma said. She pulled the cord through a small hole in one end of the shell, knotted it, and then put it around Addy's neck.

"Remember what I told you about the love you need to carry in your heart. It ain't nothing you can touch like this shell, but when you find yourself feeling sad or scared, you dip into that love, Addy. It's a well with no bottom, and it can give you strength and courage."

Addy rubbed the shell between her fingers. Its rounded top was as smooth as soap. The flat underside was also smooth, except for the middle, where the shell closed in on itself. There it felt like the teeth of a fine comb.

"My great-grandma must have been brave to come across the water all alone. I'm gonna be brave just like she was," Addy said.

"She *was* brave, Addy," Momma answered, "and you brave, too. But there's one thing different about you and your great-grandma. Her journey ended in slavery. Yours, girl, is taking you to freedom."

As Addy and Momma settled down in the cave to wait for sunset, Addy looked at the cowrie shell, thinking about the brave girl she had never met.

When night finally came, Addy and Momma started out again. The moon lit their way through the woods. As they approached the end of the trees, they heard the rushing sound of water. They had come to a wide river.

"This got to be the river near the Gifford plantation that Poppa talked about," Addy whispered.

"We got to cross it," Momma said, sounding scared.

They stuffed their hats and things in their pockets and stood on the bank of the river for a few moments, afraid to enter the foaming, angry water. Sam had taught Addy how to swim, but this water looked dangerous—and Momma didn't know how to swim at all.

Holding tight to each other, they started into the water together. Addy picked her way along the squishy bottom, her bare feet slipping on the slimy rocks that were stuck in the mud. Once she lost her balance and pulled Momma with her. Addy felt her mother's grip tighten around her hand and realized again how frightened Momma was.

Regaining their footing, they slowly made their way to the center of the river. There the current started to pull at them. It lifted them off the bottom and dragged them sideways. Hard as they tried to walk against it, the water was stronger than they were, and they were pushed farther and farther away from shore. Addy could hear Momma sputter as water filled her mouth and nose.

"Momma, keep your head up," Addy yelled as loud as she dared. "Just don't go under."

"Momma, keep your head up," Addy yelled as loud as she dared.

Suddenly a huge swell of water rushed against them, pulling Momma's hand from Addy's, dragging her away. Addy turned just in time to see her mother disappear beneath the churning water.

Addy wanted to scream, but she kept it inside. Instead, she drew in air, filling her lungs, and dove under the water. She struggled against the current, trying to stay close to the place where Momma had disappeared. She couldn't see a thing in the dark water. She felt around for Momma, but she found nothing. Addy's lungs began to burn. She was running out of air. Popping up above the water, she looked around frantically.

"Momma," she called, gulping for air. "Momma, where you at?"

Afraid no answer would come, she dove down again. This time she let the current push her while she dragged her arms through the water, searching for her mother. Suddenly, Addy was stopped by a fallen tree under the water. She groped among the branches, but their sharp ends jabbed and poked her. She kicked furiously to get away when suddenly her foot hit something soft. It was Momma, trapped in the branches. Addy braced herself against a large limb, grabbed Momma, and then pushed off against the tree with all her strength to bring both of them to the surface.

Gasping for air, the two struggled to the far shore. Clutching each other, they finally reached the shallows where the water calmed. Exhausted and breathless, they fell on the riverbank. When Addy could finally talk, she whispered, "Momma, is you all right?"

"You saved me, Addy," Momma said weakly. "You a brave girl."

Addy was shivering as she and her mother got up and slowly made their way into the woods. Their wet clothes stuck to them. Addy reached up to see if the cowrie shell was still around her neck. It was there, and something else was, too. It felt like a wet leaf. When she peeled it off, Addy realized it was a leech. She shuddered as she flicked it away.

Addy and her mother traveled for hours before Momma spotted the railroad tracks. Addy had never seen tracks before. They were shining silver, and they pointed the way north to freedom.

"These got to be the tracks your poppa talked about," Momma whispered. "We got to be extra careful out here. There ain't hardly a place to hide."

They had seen no one since they started their escape, but tracks meant a train could come at any time. Travelers might spot them. They could trust no one.

Addy and her mother followed the path of the tracks in the moonlight. When the noises of the night were gone and birdsong began to fill the air, they found a thick clump of pine trees near a curve in the tracks. Gathering dead branches and brush, they made a shelter and crawled inside.

Addy could barely keep her eyes open. She curled up and rested her head on her mother's chest.

"I'm real proud of you," Momma whispered as she gently stroked Addy's hair away from her face. Addy smiled. She could feel her mother's heart beating. It was a soothing sound.

FREEDOM TAKEN

Chapter 5

A low rumble woke Addy and her mother. Addy thought it sounded like thunder. Then a light appeared far in the distance. Addy could see it moving toward her. It looked as if the moon had fallen from the sky and was rolling through the tops of the trees. Addy and Momma crept out of their shelter just in time to see something Addy had only heard about. A train!

As it passed along a curve in the tracks, Addy watched its rear light disappear into the distance. But instead of moving away in a straight line, the train turned to the right. Addy was puzzled. Then she understood—the train had turned onto a set of tracks she could not even see yet.

"Momma, we here!" Addy said. "The safe house has to be near the place where the train turned!"

"I think you right," Momma said. "Let's go."

Addy and her mother ran hand in hand toward the place where the train had turned.

"We safe now," Addy exclaimed, a little too loudly. "We going to Philadelphia."

"Hush," Momma said sharply. "We ain't there yet."

32

"We gonna see Sam and Poppa," Addy went on. "Then we come back for Esther, and the whole family will be together again." Addy pictured them all safe in Philadelphia.

"Freedom ain't that easy, girl," warned Momma. "Don't get your hopes too high."

But Addy didn't hear her. Spurred on by her thoughts of Philadelphia, Addy moved faster and faster, pulling away from Momma. As she ran, she felt the cowrie shell beat against her chest. She was going to freedom.

It was a long way to the place where the train had turned, but Addy was still running when she saw a small light. It looked like the glow of a lantern. Addy thought it must be in the window of the safe house. She raced toward it, her mother far behind. It was not until she was closer that she saw she was wrong. She stopped suddenly. The light was from a small campfire in a clearing near the tracks. A group of men were gathered around it. Addy could see them lying on the ground, sleeping. She was about to turn and run back the other way when she heard a gruff voice call out, "Who's there?"

Addy could see the face of a white man in the light of the fire. He had on a gray jacket and a gray hat. He was a Confederate soldier—and he was staring right at her!

"Oh, it's you, boy," the soldier said.

Although Addy knew he was looking right at her, she didn't think he was talking to her. He was talking to some boy. But what boy? Just then Addy remembered the disguise. *She* was the boy!

"Bring me some water," the soldier said.

Desperately, Addy looked around. Then she saw a bucket of water. To get to it she had to walk right through the soldiers' camp. She saw another soldier on the ground stir. What if they all woke up and captured her?

Addy lowered her head, touched the cowrie shell briefly, and began to move. Inside she was shaking, but on the outside she was walking straight and strong past the sleeping soldiers. She picked up the bucket and brought it to the soldier.

Addy kept her head down while the soldier drank.

"Get on back to sleep," the soldier said.

Addy wanted to rush back into the woods, but she knew she couldn't. She acted as though she belonged in the camp. She walked to the edge of the clearing and lay down. The soldier lay down, too, and Addy waited a few minutes until she could hear him snoring. Then, as quietly as she could, Addy crept away from the soldiers and into the woods. *I got to warn Momma,* Addy thought. Just when she had gotten far enough away from the camp to start running, someone reached out and grabbed her.

It was Momma. She pulled Addy so close to her that Addy could feel the shell pressed between them. Momma held Addy for a long moment and then led her away.

When they were far from the camp, Momma spoke at last. "I was watching you with them soldiers, Addy, and I was holding my breath the whole time. You kept your feelings inside this time. Your poppa would be proud of you."

They walked farther along the tracks until they came to the place where two sets of tracks met and formed a silvery cross. A house stood just beyond the cross up on a little hill. It was white with red shutters. Poppa had been right.

Addy and her mother crouched in the shadows, staring at the white house. There was no light from inside.

"Why we waiting?" Addy whispered.

"I don't know if it's safe," her mother said.

"It's got to be safe," Addy said. "It's a safe house."

"Addy, it ain't that simple," Momma said. "There might be more of them soldiers around. I don't trust them."

"But Momma, we got to trust the white woman who live there. If we don't, where we gonna go?" Addy asked.

Without answering, Momma took a deep breath and

stood, pulling Addy up with her. They slipped out of the shadows and walked to the house.

Momma tapped lightly on the door. No answer came. She tapped again, and still there was no answer.

At last, a light glowed in the house. Through a small window, Addy could see the light of a candle move through the dark house. She heard the door being unlatched on the other side.

It opened, and an old woman not much taller than Addy stood before them. Her face shone in the light of her candle.

"Miss Caroline? Can you help us?" Addy asked.

Addy saw the woman's face twist into an angry scowl. "I thought I told you not to come here, boy. Go back and tell those soldiers I won't help them," Miss Caroline said. She started to shut the door.

Addy stuck her foot in the door to keep it from closing. "We ain't with them soldiers, ma'am," Addy said quickly, "and I ain't no boy." Addy pulled her hat off, revealing her braids. "Me and my momma running away to freedom. Can you help us?"

Addy saw the look on the woman's face soften. All the anger washed from it.

"Come in," Miss Caroline said. "Please."

Addy and her mother stepped inside. The woman

closed the door behind them and led them to the kitchen.

"My, oh my," Miss Caroline said. "Those are some fine disguises. I thought you were with those Confederate soldiers. They got here yesterday and sent a boy right over here to ask me for food. I didn't give them one crumb, but you two are welcome. Sit down and I'll start a fire."

Addy and her mother sat watching the woman work. She seemed to be everywhere, starting the fire, dragging a tin tub next to it, heating a large pot of water, putting plates on the small table.

"Let us help," Momma said.

"No, you sit and rest. I know you must be tired," Miss Caroline said. "Who sent you here?"

"Uncle Solomon," Addy's mother said. "We trying to get to Philadelphia."

The woman nodded. "I've known Solomon for over fifty years—since we were both children on farms that were next to each other." She served Addy and her mother some rice and boiled greens. While Addy and Momma ate, Miss Caroline left the kitchen and returned with a bundle.

"These are clothes I save for runaways. After your bath, you find something that fits. You can rest here tonight. Then I'll take you to the coast. You can get a ship to Philadelphia from there. We have to leave before sunup—before those soldiers wake in the morning and come back here."

"Thank you so much, ma'am," Addy's mother said. "I wish I could do something for you."

Addy went to her kerchief and untied it. She took out the half dime Uncle Solomon had given her and held it out to the woman.

"Oh, I don't want money," Miss Caroline said, filling the tub with hot water. "You both are so brave to have escaped and come so far. It's thanks enough to know I'm helping you have a new life."

Miss Caroline left Addy and her mother to take long, hot baths. The dirt from their journey melted off them. That night, for the first time ever, Addy and Momma slept on a real mattress, not one full of itchy cornhusks. Addy tried to stay awake so she could think about how good it felt to be clean and safe, but she was too tired. She fell asleep in Momma's arms.

Before the sun came up, Addy and Momma got ready to leave. Momma put on a brown dress, Addy a blue one. Addy loved her dress with its swirl of flowers and bows on the sleeves. It was prettier than any she imagined when she dreamed about freedom. Addy stood straight and tall for her mother to see.

"How I look, Momma?" Addy asked.

Momma's eyes filled with tears. "I wish your poppa could see you now, child."

The sky was barely light when Miss Caroline led Addy and her mother to a wagon outside. Momma climbed into the back and crouched low. She reached out to help Addy. Just then, Addy heard a twig snap. She and Momma both froze, and Addy held her breath. *Is it a Confederate soldier?* Addy wondered. Her heart was pounding in her chest. Momma's hand squeezed Addy's. Addy turned her head and scanned the trees. There was no sign of the soldiers. Addy exhaled.

After Addy climbed into the wagon, she and Momma lay flat. Miss Caroline covered them with some old sacks. The wagon rocked gently as it pulled away from the safe house. Addy lay close to her mother. She reached to her neck and felt for the shell. Holding it tightly, Addy thought of Esther, Sam, Poppa, and even her great-grandma who had come across the water alone. They were all with her. With the deep well of love in her heart, she could feel them with her.

"Momma, we done it," Addy said softly. "Just like Poppa said. We took our freedom."

A NEW HOME
⌒ Chapter 6 ⌒

everal days later, Addy and her mother stood on a busy pier in Philadelphia. Addy held Momma's hand and looked around nervously. *We finally in Philadelphia,* she thought. *This where Poppa say freedom is.* But instead of feeling free, Addy felt lost in a sea of strangers.

Addy had never seen so many people in her life. It seemed as if everyone in Philadelphia must be on the pier. Some people bent under the weight of heavy trunks. Others had nothing. Some people stood quietly, looking lost. Others shouted out to people who were meeting them.

"I wish Sam and Poppa was here," Addy said as she saw a small girl being swept up in a man's strong arms. "Wouldn't it be something if we was to turn around and they was here, just like magic?" Addy said.

"It would be something," Momma sighed. "I wish I knew where they was."

Addy heard sadness in Momma's voice. Addy knew Poppa and Sam were probably slaves on another plantation—unless they had been able to escape. But baby Esther was still at Master Stevens's plantation. Addy wished they

Addy held Momma's hand and looked around nervously.

had all been together when she and Momma finally made it across North Carolina to a hot, crowded boat that took them to Philadelphia.

It had been half an hour since Addy and Momma had gotten off the boat. "You think we should be waiting some-place else?" Addy asked.

"The boat captain said to wait here, Addy," Momma said. "Somebody gonna come for us."

"Maybe we should ask somebody what them signs say," Addy suggested as she looked at signs around the pier.

"We ain't gonna do that," Momma said quickly, with fear in her voice. "We in the big city now, and we can't be trusting strangers."

I wish I could read, Addy thought. *Then I could help.* But she did not know one letter. As she shifted back and forth on her aching feet, Addy began to worry. *What if no one comes?* she wondered. *Where we gonna go?*

Another ten minutes passed before Addy saw a woman and girl coming toward them. The girl was about Addy's size. She waved to Addy as if she were a long-lost friend. As she came closer, Addy saw a sunny smile on her face.

"I'm sorry we late," said the woman, who was tall and heavyset. She reached out to hug Momma and then Addy. "I was told you was coming on the *Libby*, which is way down on pier thirty-five. Come to find out, you was on the

Liberty here on pier three. I'm Mabel Moore and this is my girl, Sarah."

Sarah shook Addy's hand. "It's good meeting you," she said. Up close, her smile was even brighter.

Mrs. Moore went on, "We from the Freedom Society of Trinity A.M.E. Church, and we gonna take you to the church and help you get settled."

"We grateful," Momma said. "I'm Ruth Walker and this is my girl, Addy."

"Well, come on with us," Mrs. Moore said.

As they fell in step behind their mothers, Addy looked shyly at Sarah. Sarah's big, dark eyes were so bright, Addy could see herself in them when Sarah turned to her and asked, "Where'd you and your momma come from?"

"North Carolina," Addy answered. "We was slaves on a plantation."

"My family from Virginia. We was slaves, too," Sarah said. "My teacher, Miss Dunn, from North Carolina. Her family was slaves, too."

"They got colored people up here teaching school?" Addy asked with amazement. Back on the plantation, she didn't know any colored people who could even read.

"They sure do," Sarah said. "Miss Dunn went to college and everything. You got to be smart to do that." Sarah looked at Addy. "You is coming to school, ain't you?"

"Momma say I can go," Addy answered.

"That's good," said Sarah. "We learn to read and write. We have spelling matches and learn our sums. We even study the war. You gonna like school. You'll see."

At a busy corner, Sarah took Addy's hand. "I don't want you getting lost on your first day," she said.

Addy was glad to hold Sarah's hand as they walked down the crowded, narrow streets. Addy stared at the carts piled high with fruits and vegetables, heaps of coal, and bundles of rags. She looked up at the horse-drawn wagons and carriages that sped past them. She looked down so that she wouldn't step in garbage and horse droppings. She stared at all the people, black and white, old and young, many wearing fine clothes.

Sarah pointed to a street sign. "See that sign there?" she asked Addy. "It tell you where you at. We on Second Street now. When I come up here, I got lost loads of times because I couldn't read."

"Wish I could read," Addy mumbled.

"Miss Dunn will teach you to read," Sarah said, giving Addy's hand a reassuring squeeze. "She taught me. And I can help you learn, too."

Addy smiled at Sarah. "I'd like that," she said.

"I'm gonna help you, I promise," Sarah said, smiling her sunny smile.

⊙

When they arrived at the church, Mrs. Moore led Addy, Momma, and Sarah down to the basement and into a large meeting hall filled with people. Long tables were covered with platters of fried chicken, greens, biscuits, pies, and cakes. Addy had seen food like this only once before, when Master Stevens had a grand party. Sarah whispered to Addy that most of the people in the room were church members she knew. But some were slaves who had just arrived from the South. They were new like Addy and Momma. By the time Addy and Momma sat down to eat, it seemed they had been hugged and welcomed by everyone in the room.

While they were eating, Mrs. Moore asked Momma, "What kind of work can you do?"

"I can sew," Momma said.

Mrs. Moore's face brightened. "There's a woman over on South Street named Mrs. Ford. She a white woman, and she got a small dress shop. She can be fussy, but she pay good, and she got a room you and Addy can stay in."

After the meal, Mrs. Moore left Sarah at the church while she took Addy and Momma to the dress shop just a few blocks away. The tiny shop was crammed with cloth, thread, ribbon, yarn, feathers, and boxes. A woman sat bent over her sewing. She looked up when they arrived.

"Good day, Mrs. Ford," Mrs. Moore said. Mrs. Moore

introduced Addy and Momma and said, "I think Ruth
Walker would be a fine seamstress for you."

"I'll be the judge of that," Mrs. Ford snapped, looking
over the top of her spectacles. "The last girl you brought
here got married and left me soon after she started. I'm an
abolitionist and I want to help you colored people. But I
have a business to run, and I can't take too many chances."

"Momma a real good sewer," Addy added bravely, "and
we ain't gonna take off."

Momma squeezed Addy's arm, and Addy fell silent.

Mrs. Ford's sharp eyes looked at Addy and then at
Momma. She said, "I'll hire you, Mrs. Walker—on a trial
basis. A dollar a week to start. Most of my customers are

from Society Hill, and they expect the best. You'll have to do fine work—and make deliveries. If you can't, I won't keep you on. This is a business, not a charity ward."

"Yes, ma'am," Momma said, her voice soft but steady.

"All right then," said Mrs. Ford. "I'll take you up to the room where you and your daughter can stay."

Addy and Momma followed Mrs. Ford up three flights of steep, dark stairs. At the top was a garret. Addy's heart sank. The attic room was smaller than the cabin Addy's family had lived in back on the plantation. There was a table with two chairs, a bed, and a small stove. Then Addy saw something that made her feel better—a window that looked out over the street. Addy's cabin on the plantation had no windows.

"It's not much," Mrs. Ford said.

"It'll be fine," Momma said quickly. She put her arm around Addy's shoulders. "We gonna make it a home."

FREEDOM?

Chapter 7

Addy stood at the window of the garret, gazing out at the street below. A week had passed since she and Momma had arrived in Philadelphia, and so far, freedom wasn't the way she dreamed it would be.

Momma worked long hours in the shop, working just as hard as she had on the plantation. But back there, if Addy didn't have a chore to do, she could find Momma and sit with her. Not here. Addy had gone down to the shop on Momma's first day. But Mrs. Ford made it clear that Addy was not to be there while Momma was working.

So Addy spent her days in the hot room in the attic. Sometimes a small breeze pushed through the window, but the air was foul. Addy could smell soot, rotting garbage from the street, and the fishy scent of the harbor.

Addy didn't like being alone in the room, but she was too scared to go out by herself. She didn't know her way around. She couldn't read the street signs, and the crowds of people in the streets frightened her. The only time Addy went downstairs during the day was to go to the privy. Ten families used the same privy. It sat in the middle of a dark,

filthy alley. The privy smelled awful, and
the alley did, too. People threw all sorts
of things into the alley—dirty water, table
scraps. At night, rats prowled through the piles of garbage.

Addy had seen Sarah only once, at church on Sunday.
Sarah's mother was a washerwoman and Sarah helped her,
so she didn't have time to play. Addy longed for Esther,
Sam, and Poppa more than ever, but she didn't tell Momma.

Addy was lost in her thoughts when she heard someone
running up the stairs. She opened the door and saw Sarah.

"I'm so glad you here!" Addy exclaimed. "Ain't you got
to help your momma today?"

"I do," Sarah said. "She sent me to the store for some
bluing and a cake of soap. She said I could stop by here for
a minute. And guess what?" Sarah went on. "Your momma
said you could come with me."

Addy was so happy that she took Sarah's hand and
they ran down the stairs. When they got outside, Sarah
said eagerly, "School start next week. I can't wait."

"Me neither," Addy said excitedly.

"You can sit with me," said Sarah. "We got double
desks, and you can be my desk partner."

"Good!" agreed Addy, though she couldn't imagine
what a double desk looked like.

"My momma is letting me wear my Christmas dress

from last year to the first day of school," Sarah went on.

Addy looked down at her dress. It was the same blue one she had worn when Sarah met her at the pier.

"Do the girls dress real fancy at school?" she asked.

"Some do," Sarah answered. "There's this one girl named Harriet. She got lots of pretty dresses."

"It sound like she rich," Addy said.

"Compared to us she is," Sarah replied. "Her momma don't work."

They came to a curb and waited for a wagon to go by. Addy had never seen anything like it. The wagon was packed with people, some sitting, some standing.

"What kind of wagon is that?" Addy asked.

"It's a streetcar," Sarah explained. "Streetcars go all over the city to take people to different places."

"Let's get on it," Addy said as they crossed the street. "It look like fun."

"We can't ride it," Sarah said, "even if we had money for the fare, which we don't."

"You mean children got to ride with their momma or poppa?" Addy asked.

"No," Sarah said. "I mean they don't let colored people ride on that streetcar."

Addy looked confused.

"It's true," Sarah said. "There is a few streetcars for colored people to ride on. But we can only ride on the outside platform, even if it's raining or snowing. And they charge us colored folks the same fare they charge whites."

"That ain't right," Addy said.

"It ain't, but it's the way things is," Sarah said.

When Momma came to bed that night, Addy told her about the streetcars. "This where freedom supposed to be at," Addy said. "There ain't supposed to be things colored folks can't do."

"Honey, you right," Momma said, turning over the pillow so the cool side touched Addy's cheek. "But there's more to freedom than riding a streetcar. There ain't nobody here that own us, and beat us, and work us like animals. I got me a paying job. You can go to school and learn to read and write. When you got an education, you got a freedom nobody can take from you. You'll still have it even if you never ride a streetcar."

"I wish you ain't have to work so hard," Addy said.

"We got to buy everything now," Momma said. "We need money for food and candles and coal and matches."

Addy sighed. "And it all cost so much."

"Freedom got a cost," Momma nodded. "Just like Uncle

Solomon told us before we left the plantation. It cost money and hard work and heartache." She kissed Addy's forehead. "Be patient, honey. Things gonna get better, I promise. Now, you go on to sleep. I got sewing to do."

The first day of school, Momma and Addy were both up before the sun. Momma had washed, starched, and ironed Addy's blue dress so that it looked like new. Now she braided Addy's hair in two braids and tied each with a ribbon that Mrs. Ford had given her from the end of a roll.

When Momma finished, she hugged Addy. "Do good in school now, Addy," she said. "You a smart girl."

"I'm gonna work hard, Momma," Addy replied as she hugged Momma back. Suddenly they heard someone running up the stairs.

Sarah burst into the room. "You ready, Addy?" she asked. Sarah had on a dark green dress trimmed in white. It was old, but clean and carefully mended.

"You look real nice, Sarah," Momma said. She handed Addy her lunch pail. Momma had tied a scrap of green and white cloth to the pail so Addy could tell hers  from other children's. Momma walked downstairs with the girls. "Y'all be careful now. Watch out for them wagons and streetcars. Go straight to school and come right straight back here after."

"Don't worry, Mrs. Walker," Sarah said. She hooked arms with Addy. "I'm gonna look after Addy."

The Sixth Street School was a brick building near Trinity Church. Boys and girls had gathered on the steps out front. All of them were black, and they were all different ages. Addy felt scared, but she tried not to show it. She held tight to Sarah's hand as they walked past the other students and went into the building.

Addy felt more nervous than ever when she saw their classroom. It was crammed with desks. In one corner was a large black stove. On two walls of the room were huge black squares filled with writing. On another wall there was a large piece of paper filled with colorful shapes. *What's that for?* Addy wondered.

Sarah's voice interrupted Addy's thoughts. "Here come Miss Dunn," Sarah said.

Addy watched as the teacher entered the room. Miss Dunn held her head high and her back straight. Her long skirts swung gracefully as she made her way across the room. She seemed to be gliding on air.

Miss Dunn smiled at Addy and Sarah. "Welcome back, Sarah," she said. "And who is your friend?"

"This is Addy," Sarah answered. "She from North Carolina just like you. She ain't never been to school before."

Miss Dunn put her hand on Addy's shoulder. "I'm so

pleased you're here, Addy," she said. "You know, I never went to school until my family came north. When I started, some things seemed a little strange. You might feel a bit confused this first week, but you'll soon learn your way. I know Sarah will help you."

Addy smiled as Miss Dunn floated away. The teacher had made her feel much better. Addy and Sarah sat down together at a double desk at the back of the room.

When everyone was seated, Miss Dunn said, "Good morning, boys and girls. I am Miss Dunn." She pointed to her name on the blackboard. "I know many of you, but I see some new faces." Miss Dunn asked every student to stand up and state his or her name. When it was Addy's turn, she said her name softly.

After everyone had taken a turn, Miss Dunn said, "I know we will enjoy our year together. I want you children who have been here before to help the new students. I will assign permanent desk partners tomorrow."

Then she announced that the class would spend the morning copying from the board. "Sarah," she said, "please help Addy copy the alphabet."

Sarah was a patient teacher. She showed Addy how to hold her slate pencil and how to form the letters of the alphabet. Addy tried to hold her pencil the way Sarah did, but it kept slipping. Addy finally wrapped her entire hand around the pencil. Even then, the letters she slowly formed were squiggly and rough.

Miss Dunn stopped to look at Addy's slate. "You're doing fine," she said. Then she wrote something on one side of the slate. "This is your name," she said.

Addy stared at the letters. It was the first time in her life that she had seen her name written down. Addy tried to copy the letters carefully. But her writing wobbled across her side of the slate in a crooked row. Addy erased them and started again. This time they looked more like Miss Dunn's letters.

Sarah looked at Addy's slate. "I can read that plain as day," she said kindly. "A-D-D-Y."

Addy smiled. It had been a struggle, but she had written her own name, just as she dreamed she would. And she had found something she had not even dreamed of when she worked in the tobacco fields. In Sarah, she had found a friend.

TESTED
~ Chapter 8 ~

he next morning, Miss Dunn announced the new seat assignments. "Addy Walker, you'll share a desk with Harriet Davis," she said.

Addy and Sarah looked at each other, and Sarah said, "Miss Dunn, can Addy stay with me? I been helping her."

"No, Sarah, I want Addy to sit near the front of the room. Clara Johnson will be your new desk partner. You can help her," Miss Dunn replied.

Addy rose slowly and went to her new seat. She smiled shyly, but Harriet did not smile back.

Harriet had light brown skin, and she wore her hair loose. She had on the most beautiful dress Addy had ever seen. It was yellow and trimmed with rows of lace. Addy realized that this must be the girl Sarah had told her about.

"Do you know the alphabet?" Harriet asked.

"I'm just learning it," Addy answered. "Sarah was teaching me."

A quick frown crossed Harriet's face. "Sarah? Sarah can hardly read herself! I'll help you. I taught myself to read when I was four. Miss Dunn put you with me because I'm

"Miss Dunn put you with me because
I'm the smartest one in the class," Harriet said.

the smartest one in the class."

"Sarah smart, too," Addy responded.

Harriet ignored her comment. "I'm named after Harriet Tubman. She helped run the Underground Railroad. You probably didn't know that. I know plenty of things like that."

At lunch Sarah asked, "How you like sitting with Harriet?"

"She real smart and she got fine clothes just like you said. I wish I had a dress as pretty as the one she has on," Addy said.

"You know how much one of them fancy dresses cost?" Sarah asked.

"How much?" Addy asked.

"More than my momma and poppa make in a whole month," Sarah answered. "Your momma can't afford to make you a dress like that, Addy."

Addy's eyes opened wide. She had no idea one dress could cost so much. "Maybe my momma can find a way."

"I'm sick of talking about Harriet," Sarah snapped.

Addy was surprised by Sarah's reaction. "What's the matter?" she asked. "Don't you like her?"

"That ain't it," Sarah said, letting out a sigh. "Addy, Harriet don't like me. She all stuck-up. She think she better than other people. If your family ain't got no money, she don't like you. And you know my family poor."

"But Harriet was nice to me," Addy protested, "and she know my family is poor."

"Listen, Addy. She was only nice 'cause Miss Dunn told her to be," Sarah said firmly. "Harriet don't have no poor girls like us for her friends. She gonna try to make you her slave. She tried it with me when I came to school last year, but I wouldn't let her. That's why she don't like me. She gonna hurt you just like she hurt me last year."

"Well, maybe Harriet changed from when you first come up here," Addy said hopefully. "Harriet say she got plenty to teach me, and I got plenty to learn."

As the weeks passed, Addy's fascination with Harriet grew. Every day Harriet wore a beautiful dress. Each one seemed brand-new. And schoolwork came so easily to Harriet! She was always the first one in the class to finish her lesson.

Addy worked very hard, and so she was discouraged after her first spelling test. Out of the twenty words on the test, Addy spelled twelve wrong. But Miss Dunn was encouraging. "Look how many words you got right, Addy. If you keep learning this fast, you'll be one of the best spellers in the class. Maybe your mother could help you with the words you missed."

"Yes, ma'am," Addy said softly. She didn't want to tell

Miss Dunn that Momma couldn't read or write. And she didn't want Harriet to overhear her say it.

When Addy and Sarah were walking home after school, Addy said, "I ain't never gonna catch up. Younger girls can read and spell better than me. Maybe it's too late for me to learn."

"It ain't never too late," said Sarah. "You can't learn everything at once. Learning go slow. I didn't do so good on the test, neither. I should've studied harder."

"I studied hard and I still didn't do good," Addy said. "How many did you get right?"

"How many did you get right?" Sarah asked.

"I asked first," Addy said.

"Well, I got 'em all wrong 'cause I didn't study at all," Sarah said. "My poppa can't hardly find work, so my momma and me been taking in extra washing. Sometimes I ain't got time to do my lessons."

"Maybe we can do our lessons together," Addy said.

"I'd like that," Sarah said, sounding more cheerful.

Sarah left Addy at the door of Mrs. Ford's shop, and Addy stepped inside. As she headed toward the stairs, she saw Momma sitting in the back of the shop. She was crying. "What's the matter, Momma?" Addy asked.

Momma dried her eyes on the sleeve of her dress. "You can come in, Addy," she said. "Mrs. Ford ain't here.

She went out and left these packages for me to deliver. She wrote down the addresses on this here paper. I ain't dare tell her I can't read. She gonna be coming back soon expecting to see these packages gone, but I don't know where to take them."

"I can take them," Addy said. She looked at the addresses, but her heart sank when she realized she could read only one of them. Then an idea came to her. "Momma, Sarah can help. She can read way better than me, and she know her way around Philadelphia. Let me go catch up with Sarah. It's the only way," Addy begged.

"All right," Momma said after a moment. "But y'all be extra careful."

Addy grabbed the packages and the paper and ran. She caught up with Sarah a few blocks away and explained the problem. Sarah studied the paper for a moment. Then she said, "I know where these streets is. Let's go."

Sarah hurried through the busy streets with Addy rushing along beside her. Sarah pointed to the street signs and read the names aloud. She showed Addy how the numbers on the houses went in order. After they had delivered the last package, the girls headed back to the shop.

As they walked in the door, Momma threw her arms around them. "Sarah, you been a big help. I don't know what we'd do without you," she said.

Just then Mrs. Ford returned. When she saw Addy and Sarah, she said, "What's going on here, Mrs. Walker? This is a place of business, you know."

"Yes, ma'am. The girls were just leaving," Momma said quickly. Sarah headed for home, and Addy hurried up the stairs to the garret.

That evening, as Momma was cooking supper, she sounded worried. "I ain't got a right to this job because I ain't been honest with Mrs. Ford. I gotta learn to read or find something else to do."

"I can teach you how to read!" Addy exclaimed.

Momma shook her head. "It's too late for me," she said.

"Sarah say it ain't never too late," said Addy. She took her spelling paper out of her satchel. "I got most of the words wrong, but Miss Dunn say if you help me, I could be one of the best spellers at school."

"But I don't know how to help you, Addy," Momma replied. "I don't know the letters."

"I can teach them to you," Addy answered, "and I'll get practice from helping you."

Momma looked at the cowrie shell hanging around Addy's neck—the shell that had come from Addy's great-grandmother, who had been brought to America as a slave. Then Momma looked into Addy's eyes. "All right, Addy. I'll try," said Momma. "Our family done faced tougher things than this. Ain't no change coming overnight, but by and by, maybe we'll both learn."

Addy smiled. "Let's have our first lesson tonight."

As weeks passed and it started to get cold, Momma kept a small fire in the stove in the evenings. Sometimes when they made bread for supper, Addy showed Momma how to spell words by forming letters with scraps of

leftover dough. Momma loved to write *Sam, Poppa,* and *Esther.* "Seeing their names make me feel closer to them," she said. After they ate, they went over Addy's lessons. Addy taught Momma how to count, showing Momma what she had learned at school by using beans.

Every day Addy and Sarah went to and came home from school together. Sarah taught Addy how to read the names on street signs and shops as they walked along. One brisk morning as they passed a grocery store, Addy stopped to read the sign. "Eggs forty-eight cents a dozen."

"That's right," Sarah said. "You getting real smart."

"You been a good teacher," Addy said, smiling at her friend. "But you and me not as smart as Harriet. You should see her papers. All hundreds."

Sarah didn't say anything.

"Did you see that blue dress Harriet had on yesterday?" Addy sighed. "It was *so* pretty. I never even seen her in it before. She must have ten or fifteen dresses."

"Let's talk about something else," Sarah cut in. "I don't like talking about her, or even thinking about her."

But Addy liked thinking about Harriet. Harriet had everything that Addy had dreamed freedom would bring *her.* Harriet had fancy dresses. Harriet was smart. Harriet was sure of herself. When they were at their desk together, Harriet helped Addy with her schoolwork. But Harriet never invited Addy to be part of her group. Harriet had many friends. Her friends wore fancy dresses and matching hair ribbons. They buzzed around Harriet as if she were a queen bee. They ate lunch together and played at recess. Addy and Sarah walked home the same way Harriet and her friends did, but Addy and Sarah were never asked to join them.

One day at the end of October, Harriet and her friends were walking home just ahead of Addy and Sarah. Addy started walking faster.

"What you hurrying up for?" Sarah asked sharply.

Addy whispered back, "Let's catch up with them."

"You can if you want," Sarah answered, "but I ain't walking with them."

"Aw, come on. We all going the same way," Addy said softly, catching hold of Sarah's arm.

"I said I ain't walking with them," Sarah repeated loudly.

Harriet stopped and turned around. "I heard you, Sarah," she snapped. "Nobody *asked* you to walk with us." Harriet smiled a cool smile at Addy. "But *you* can come with us if you want, Addy."

Addy got a warm, excited feeling. She turned to look at Sarah, but Sarah wouldn't look at her. Sarah looked down at her scuffed boots. Addy didn't know what to do. She knew she would hurt Sarah if she went with Harriet.

"Sarah isn't the boss of you," Harriet said in a loud voice as Addy hesitated. "You can walk with us whenever you want, Addy. It's your decision." Harriet gave Sarah a nasty look, and then she and her friends disappeared around the corner.

THE LINES ARE DRAWN
∾ Chapter 9 ∾

That evening, Addy and Momma made supper together. Momma sprinkled flour on the table and began rolling out a piece of dough. She was making biscuits to go with their supper of black-eyed peas. Addy gathered scraps of dough as Momma began cutting the biscuits.

"One word I been wanting to learn to spell is *family*," Momma said to Addy.

"I know how to spell that word," Addy answered. She started working the scraps of dough into thin strips and made an F and then an A. "Momma, what you think Esther doing right now?" Addy asked as she continued making the letters.

"I suspect she getting ready to eat her supper, too," Momma said.

"I miss her," Addy said, "and Poppa and Sam." She sighed deeply. "Momma, when we gonna live together again like a real family?"

Momma sighed, too. "I can't say when we'll be together again, Addy," she said. "But I don't want you thinking that we ain't a family 'cause we ain't all in one place. We just as much a family as we was back in North Carolina."

Addy finished spelling *family* with the dough pieces.

"F-A-M-I-L-Y," Momma read. "Family, that's us."

"That's us." Addy smiled softly.

The next day in school, Miss Dunn talked about the war and about the progress the soldiers from the North were making. "It appears that our Union troops are winning the war," she said proudly.

Addy turned to Harriet and said, "My brother wanted to fight in the war."

"Really?" replied Harriet. She didn't sound interested. "My uncle is serving with the Third Infantry. That was the first colored regiment organized in the state."

"Oh," said Addy. She wished she knew as much about where Sam was as Harriet knew about her uncle.

Sarah raised her hand. "Miss Dunn, why there got to be a war at all?" she asked.

Miss Dunn paused for a moment. "Sometimes people fight even when they don't want to. They fight for what they believe is right," she said.

"I still wish there wasn't no war," Sarah said.

Before Miss Dunn could respond, Harriet turned around in her seat and said to Sarah, "You know the war is going to free the slaves. You should be glad for the war. *You* were a slave yourself."

"Harriet, that will be enough," Miss Dunn said. "Almost all of us colored people used to be slaves."

"Not me," Harriet said proudly. "My family has always been free."

Addy saw a tense look come over Miss Dunn's face.

"Girls and boys, almost all colored people came to America as slaves," Miss Dunn said. "If you weren't a slave, someone in your family probably was. One of the reasons there is a war now is because a line exists between colored and white people. That line is slavery." Miss Dunn turned to Harriet. "We don't need to do or say anything that draws more lines between people. The entire country has been divided in two. Let's not make differences based on who was a slave or wasn't, or *anything* else. Is that clear, class?"

"Yes, Miss Dunn," all the students answered together.

"Harriet," Miss Dunn said, "do I make myself clear?"

"Yes, ma'am," Harriet mumbled, embarrassed.

"Good," said Miss Dunn.

When school ended that day, Harriet put her arm around Addy's shoulders. "Are you walking home with me and my friends, or do you have to ask Sarah's permission?"

"I don't have to ask her permission," Addy said quickly. "I'm gonna walk with you."

"Good," Harriet said. She sounded satisfied.

Addy gathered her lunch pail and books and went to Sarah's desk. "I'm gonna walk with Harriet today," Addy said firmly. "She asked me. You can come, too, if you want."

"No, I can't," Sarah said, her voice shaking.

Addy could see that Sarah was hurt. She was starting to say something to Sarah when she heard Harriet call, "Come on, Addy."

"Go on," Sarah said bitterly. "You know you want to."

Addy ran to join Harriet and her friends, but she glanced back at Sarah, who was alone. Addy felt torn.

"How do you think you'll do in the spelling match on Friday?" Harriet asked Addy.

"I hope I'm gonna do all right," Addy replied. "I been studying real hard."

"Can you believe Miss Dunn gave us seventy-five words to learn?" asked Mavis, one of Harriet's friends.

"Harriet is going to win," another girl said. "She doesn't even have to study."

"We've been going to my house after school to study for the spelling match," Harriet said. "Maybe you can come with us sometime, Addy. Here." Harriet handed Addy her books. One by one, the other girls piled their books on top.

"Why I got to carry them all?" Addy asked.

"Well, if you want to be with us, you have to be our flunky," Harriet said.

"What's that?" Addy asked, struggling with the heavy stack of books.

Harriet and her friends giggled. "Oh, Addy, I can tell that you just got off the plantation," said Harriet. "You have to be a flunky because you are the new girl. It's sort of like you have to pass a test to be friends with us."

"What kinda test?" Addy asked.

"Oh, I can't tell you too much. That would be cheating," Harriet answered.

The girls all laughed again, and Addy felt too embarrassed to ask more. She felt that the girls all had a secret that they weren't sharing with her.

When the group reached Mrs. Ford's shop, the girls quickly took their books off Addy's pile.

"I'll see y'all tomorrow," Addy called.

The girls walked away. "Bye," Harriet called, not bothering to look back at Addy.

Inside the shop, Momma and Mrs. Ford were working.

"Good afternoon, Mrs. Ford," Addy said. "I know this is a place of business, but can I talk to Momma for a minute, please?"

"Make it quick," Mrs. Ford said without looking up from her work.

"Momma, can I go to Harriet's house to study for the spelling match?" Addy asked. "I told you about her before. She my desk partner, and she invited me."

"I suppose it'd be fine," Momma answered, "but only if Sarah go with you."

Addy suddenly felt sick to her stomach. Harriet would never include her if Sarah had to come along.

"Where is your friend?" Mrs. Ford asked.

Addy looked away. "She ain't want to walk with me today," she said.

"That don't sound like Sarah," Momma said.

"It's true, Momma," Addy said quickly. "Anyhow, I know my way around now."

As Addy slowly climbed the stairs to the garret, she tried to convince herself that what she had just told Momma *was* true. Sarah had *not* wanted to walk with her today. She also tried to figure out a way she could go to Harriet's without Sarah. Addy knew a line had been drawn between Sarah and Harriet and neither one would cross it.

THE SPELLING MATCH

Chapter 10

The next morning, Addy and Sarah walked most of the way to school in silence. Finally, Addy asked, "You angry with me?"

"I ain't angry," Sarah said.

They walked the rest of the way to school without talking. As soon as they arrived, Addy hurried to her desk. Harriet was already sitting there.

"My momma say I could come to your house to study," Addy said happily.

"Well, maybe," Harriet said.

All day Addy felt jumpy with excitement. She kept thinking about the fine house Harriet must have, filled with dolls and other toys. Maybe Harriet would let her play with them this afternoon.

When the day was finally over, Sarah came up to Addy. "You ready to walk home?" she asked.

"Well . . . I'm walking with Harriet," Addy said. "I'm going to her house."

"Fine," Sarah said flatly. "Go with her. I don't care." She turned away from Addy.

"Sarah," Addy began. But Harriet's friends surrounded her. The girls dumped their books in Addy's arms again. They were every bit as heavy as the water bucket she used to carry back on the plantation. But Addy didn't complain. At last, she was going to Harriet's house.

"Did you see Sarah today?" Harriet said in a mean voice. "Her dress was so wrinkled, it looked like she slept in it."

Mavis added, "And she had a big brown stain on the front of it."

"Her mother is a washerwoman, and she can't even keep Sarah's clothes clean," said Harriet.

All the girls laughed, except Addy. "That's not funny," she said. "Her momma work hard."

"She must not be working hard enough, because Sarah is a mess," Harriet said.

"That don't matter," Addy said softly.

Harriet said, "Of course it matters. Anyway, what do you care about Sarah, Addy? You're on our side now. At least your mother keeps you looking presentable, even if you do wear that same old dress every day. Don't you have any others?"

"No," Addy said, swallowing hard.

"Addy looks good enough to be our flunky, though," Mavis said.

The girls all giggled. "That's true," Harriet said lightly. "Sarah didn't. But you, Addy, are a perfect flunky."

Addy smiled weakly, but she had a sick feeling in her stomach.

When the girls reached Mrs. Ford's shop, Harriet suddenly took her books from the pile Addy was carrying. Addy was confused. "Hey, I can go with y'all today," she said. "I can study at your house, Harriet."

"I don't think so. Not today," Harriet said.

"But the spelling match is tomorrow," Addy protested.

Harriet shrugged. "Well, maybe you can come someday, but not today," she repeated. "Come on," she said to the other girls. They grabbed their books and hurried away, leaving Addy alone at the shop door.

Addy stood there, unable to move. Finally, she ran up to the garret and threw herself on the bed. Her face burned as if she had been stung by a swarm of bees. Sarah had been right. Harriet did not want Addy to be her friend. She just wanted Addy to be her slave. And even worse, Addy had chosen to be her slave. Addy reached for the cowrie shell Momma had given her and cried with shame.

The next day was the day of the spelling match. When Addy got up, she looked for the dress that Momma always laid out over the back of her chair, but her dress wasn't there. In its place were a new blue skirt and jacket trimmed in black braid and a crisp white shirt.

"I made them out of some leftover cloth from the shop. I want you to look your best for that spelling match," Momma said, smiling. "You surprised?"

"Oh, Momma, thank you," Addy said, throwing her arms around her mother.

"I been staying up late for weeks now working on them," Momma explained as Addy got dressed. Momma's dark eyes sparkled with pride. "Look at you! You look like a fancy city girl," Momma said. "No matter how you do in the spelling match, I'm gonna be proud of you. You done worked real hard."

But as Addy walked to school that morning, she didn't feel she deserved the new clothes. She became more and more nervous during the morning lessons. When the spelling match finally started, her stomach felt queasy.

Harriet was given the first word to spell—*carriage*. She rattled off the letters quickly, "C-A-R-R-I-A-G-E."

"Correct," Miss Dunn said. "Sarah, you have the next word. Spell *button*."

"B-U-T-T-O-N," Sarah spelled in a soft voice.

"Correct," said Miss Dunn. "Addy, it's your turn. Spell *tomorrow*."

"T-O-M-O-R-O-," Addy started to spell quickly, just

as Harriet had. But then she stopped. This was one of the words she had trouble spelling. She stopped and thought. She knew she could spell this word. She started again, this time more slowly, "T-O-M-O-R-R-O-W."

"Correct," Miss Dunn said.

Addy breathed a sigh of relief. At least she wouldn't make a mistake in the first round of the spelling match.

Harriet leaned over and whispered, "I'm going to win, and my mother said I can have friends over after school for ice cream to celebrate. I might ask you."

Addy said nothing. Her stomach felt worse.

After two rounds, half the class had missed a spelling word and had to sit down. Addy was glad that Sarah was still in the contest.

Sarah's next word was *account.*

Sarah began, "A-C-C-," and then she paused. "A-C-C-O-N-T," she said.

"I'm sorry," Miss Dunn said. "That's not correct."

Addy's turn was next. She took a deep breath and spelled the word correctly. The spelling match went into the third round. Addy spelled *bridge* correctly. In the fourth round, she got *scissors* right. When the fifth round came, there were two spellers left: Harriet and Addy.

Harriet had the first word. *"Principle,"* Miss Dunn said. "We all live our lives by principles. *Principle.*"

"P-R-I-N-S-I-P-L-E," Harriet said quickly.

"I'm sorry," Miss Dunn said. "That is not correct. Addy, you must spell the word correctly to win. *Principle*."

Slowly and deliberately, Addy spelled out the letters, "P-R-I-N-C-I-P-L-E."

"Correct!" Miss Dunn exclaimed. "Addy Walker, you have truly earned this prize."

Miss Dunn came over to Addy and pinned a medal on her jacket. "Your hard work has paid off," she said.

It was time for lunch by then, and Miss Dunn announced that the class could eat outside because it was a warm day. Several girls rushed up to Addy to congratulate her before they left the classroom.

Harriet stood at the edge of the group. "Well," she said briskly. "If I had studied at all, I would have beaten you. Anyway, Miss Dunn gave you easier words."

"You're just jealous, Harriet," Mavis said. "Addy spelled the word *you* missed."

"I'm not jealous of her," Harriet insisted. Then she turned and went outside.

Mavis smiled at Addy, "You have on such a pretty new outfit. Where did your mother buy it?"

"She ain't buy it, she made it," Addy answered.

"It's nice," Mavis said before following Harriet outside.

Addy sat down at her desk, pretending she was looking

for something inside it. She felt a hand on her shoulder. It was Miss Dunn.

"This is a very special day for you, Addy. Why are you in here all by yourself?" the teacher asked.

Addy kept rooting through her desk.

"I don't think you'll find what you're looking for inside that desk, Addy," Miss Dunn said.

Addy still did not look up.

Miss Dunn reached for Addy's hand. "Addy, look at me," she said gently. Addy slowly looked up. "I suspect you're feeling bad because lines have been drawn between some girls in this class."

"Miss Dunn," Addy said, "I don't know how to get rid of the lines. I done hurt Sarah, and I wouldn't blame her if she never spoke to me again."

"We all make mistakes," Miss Dunn said. "I suspect you've learned a lesson about friendship. But you can't make things better by hiding in here. You need to think about what you stand for and act on it." Miss Dunn smiled at Addy and then left her alone.

Addy took her lunch pail from the floor, opened the lid, and looked to see what Momma had packed. When she saw what was on top, she closed the lid and hurried out of the classroom. Addy went around to the side of the building. She stopped when she saw Sarah sitting alone under a small tree. Addy took a deep breath. Then she walked up to Sarah and knelt beside her.

"I'm so sorry, Sarah," Addy said. "I wanted to be friends with Harriet because she was popular and smart and rich. But she ain't a real friend. I know you is. I never meant to hurt you. Please forgive me."

"I forgive you," Sarah said, smiling that sunny smile Addy had seen the first day she and Momma had arrived at the pier. "I wanted you to win so bad," Sarah said.

"I wanted you to win, too. I was sad when you missed your word," Addy said. "Maybe we can study spelling together right nc w." She reached into her lunch pail. There on top were four cookies Momma had made, each in the shape of a letter. L-O-V-E.

"Here," Addy said, holding the cookies on her out-stretched hand. "This is our first word."

WINDS OF WINTER
⌒ Chapter 11 ⌒

Addy knew that winter had come to Philadelphia even before she opened her eyes. It was late November, and an icy wind whistled through the crack in the garret window. Momma had just gotten up, letting a puff of cold air in the bed when she lifted the heavy quilt. But her place was still warm, so Addy snuggled into it.

Momma called to her. "Addy, honey, I need your help over here. Snow's coming right in through the window."

In the dim gray light of morning, Addy saw Momma straining to close the window. Its panes were white with frost. A little pile of snow had built up on the windowsill, and more snow had blown across the floor.

Addy got out of bed and shivered over to the window. She and Momma pulled down on the window, struggling to close it. But the window wouldn't budge.

"Go get them rags next to the stove," Momma said.

Addy got the rags and returned to Momma.

"Help me stuff these in the crack," Momma said as she poked the rags between the window and the sill. "These rags is all we got to keep the wind from coming in."

Addy put one cold foot on top of the other to try to warm up her feet. "Can't we light the stove this morning, Momma?" she asked. "It's so cold in here."

"No, honey," Momma said. "We got just enough coal to last us the week if we use it only for cooking supper." She gave Addy a warm hug. "Now you hustle to wash up. Then you won't feel the cold so bad."

Addy splashed icy cold water from the basin over her face and dressed quickly. She wrapped her shawl around her shoulders and sat down at the table. Addy crumbled cornbread in a bowl and poured buttermilk over it. As she ate, Addy spied a pile of fabric folded neatly on Momma's chair, with a spool of thread and a pair of scissors on top.

"Was you up late again sewing, Momma?" asked Addy.

Momma nodded. "I got to finish this dress for Mrs. Howell. Mrs. Ford say Mrs. Howell is real particular." Momma unfolded the fabric and looked at what she had sewn last night. "It's hard to see my stitches by candlelight. We sure do need that lamp we been saving for."

"Can I count the money again?" Addy asked.

Momma nodded. "Sure, but I ain't put nothing in the milk bottle since last week."

"I put my tips in last Saturday," Addy said proudly. "I got two big tips when I delivered them dresses to Society Hill for Mrs. Ford."

"That's good, Addy," said Momma. She reached into their hiding place behind the stove, picked up the milk bottle, and handed it to Addy. Addy turned the bottle upside down and shook it so that the coins poured out. Then she carefully counted the pennies, half dimes, and dimes.

"We got one dollar and fifty-seven cents," Addy announced.

"That ain't enough for a lamp," said Momma. "We gonna have to wait a little longer. Just hope I don't have to pull them stitches out of one of them seams in that dress."

Addy looked at the thick folds of green and red plaid taffeta that lay over the chair next to her. "Them rich girls sure got pretty dresses," she said.

"Sure do," said Momma. "Isabella Howell's gonna wear that one to some fancy Christmas party."

Addy finished her breakfast and washed her bowl and spoon in the bucket of water that stood by the stove. Then she sat down so Momma could brush and braid her hair. "Remember last Christmas, Momma?" asked Addy. She thought back to last year when she and Momma were on the plantation with Poppa, Sam, and Esther. "You made sweet-potato pudding."

"I remember," Momma said. "Sam liked my sweet-potato pudding."

"And Poppa did, too," Addy said, missing Poppa and Sam. "Sweet-potato pudding was Poppa's favorite."

"I'm gonna make that pudding for Christmas again this year," Momma said gently. "We'll take it to the church dinner. I'm sure Auntie Lula gonna be making it this year, too. So when we have Christmas dinner, we'll be eating the same thing as Auntie Lula, Uncle Solomon, and Esther."

"Last night I dreamed we was all together. Sam, Poppa, Esther—all of us here in Philadelphia," said Addy. She looked at Momma, who looked sad. "It ain't gonna be just a dream, is it, Momma?" Addy asked hopefully. "Ain't we all gonna be together someday?"

"Someday, honey. Someday. That dream keep me going. That and your bright face." Momma finished Addy's hair and leaned over to kiss the top of her head.

On the way to school that morning, Addy asked Sarah what the Christmas celebration was like at church.

"Last year, the altar was decorated with pine branches. In the middle was a manger with baby Jesus, and Mary and Joseph kneeling next to it," Sarah explained. "Lots of candles was on the altar. The whole church was glowing and beautiful."

Addy could barely imagine something so lovely.

Sarah went on, "After the service, we go downstairs for

"Last night I dreamed we was all together. Sam, Poppa, Esther—
all of us here in Philadelphia," said Addy.

Christmas dinner. Everybody bring something to share, and everyone sit down like one great big family. After dinner, there's a special shadow play for children."

"What's that?" asked Addy.

"We sit in a dark room that has a big sheet hanging in the front," said Sarah. "Behind it, there's this bright lamp. People in front of the lamp make shadows on the sheet. They act out the Christmas story while it's read out loud."

"I bet it's real nice," Addy said.

"And this year my momma's letting me sing in the children's choir." Sarah said excitedly. "You should join, too. We practice every Saturday till Christmas."

"I wish I could," said Addy. "But Saturday is when I work for Mrs. Ford. I'm doing errands and deliveries so she and Momma can spend all their time sewing."

"Well, don't worry, Addy," said Sarah kindly. "I'll teach you the songs. Then you can sing on Christmas along with everyone else."

"I'd like that," said Addy. She smiled at her friend.

"We can start right now," said Sarah. "The first song we always sing is 'Joy to the World.' Here's how it goes." With that, Sarah began to sing. Addy listened and then hummed along. Soon she knew the words.

"Joy to the world!" the two girls sang together as they hurried through the winter streets to school.

SOMETHING PRETTY

Early on Saturday morning, Addy set out on her errands and deliveries for Mrs. Ford. She stepped around the slush and dirty puddles in the street to bring a bill to a customer on Society Hill. Then she went to the dry goods store a few blocks away to pick up supplies that Mrs. Ford had ordered.

On the way to her next stop, Addy passed the windows of Mr. Delmonte's Secondhand Shop. Sometimes she and Momma went there to look for clothes or pots and pans. The socks Addy had on today had come from the secondhand shop. There was a small darn in the heel of one sock, but the other was as good as new.

Addy stopped for a minute to look in the window. Lying among the used shoes, wool caps, and old belts was a bright patch of red cloth. It looked like the corner of a scarf, but most of it was hidden behind a rusty teakettle. Addy went inside to take a closer look.

Mr. Delmonte recognized her right away. "Good morning, Addy," he said in his jolly way. "What brings you here today?"

"Can I see that red scarf in the window?" Addy asked.

Mr. Delmonte reached into the window display and moved the teakettle so he could lift out the scarf and hand it to Addy. "It's a beauty," he said. "Hardly looks worn."

Addy held the scarf to her cheek. The red fabric was soft and smooth. Right then she knew she wanted Momma to have the scarf. *Momma should have something pretty like this,* thought Addy. *She work so hard. She'd look so beautiful in this when we go to the Christmas service at church.* Addy was almost afraid to ask about the price, but she looked up at Mr. Delmonte.

"How much it cost?" she asked.

"Twenty cents," answered Mr. Delmonte. "It's a good price for something that looks like new."

Addy was discouraged. She didn't have twenty cents. But she had to buy that scarf somehow.

"Please, Mr. Delmonte," she said, "could you put it away for me? I'm gonna try my best to get the money to buy it."

"Well, I'll put it back behind that rusty kettle again," answered Mr. Delmonte. "You're the only person who's spotted it since I put it in the window last week. It will probably stay there a little longer."

"I hope so," said Addy as she carefully folded the scarf and handed it back to Mr. Delmonte.

The feel of the scarf's soft red material stayed in Addy's mind as she headed back to Mrs. Ford's shop. *How am I gonna get twenty cents?* she wondered.

Back at the shop, Mrs. Ford had three packages for her to deliver, all wrapped in brown paper. "These go to Society Hill," said Mrs. Ford as she handed them to Addy. "Be careful. Don't splash mud on them."

"Yes, ma'am," said Addy. Since Momma had worked so hard, Addy would make sure the dresses were delivered in perfect condition.

As Addy walked toward the last delivery on Spruce Street, she saw an old man lighting the street lamps. The lamps cast a golden glow on the wet sidewalks. When Addy got to the house, she rang the bell and waited for the big door to open. A maid finally came, and Addy handed her the last bundle.

"This is from Mrs. Ford's shop," she said proudly.

The maid took the package and handed Addy five pennies. Addy thanked her and turned away. As she walked back down Spruce Street, she curled her fingers around the coins inside her mitten.

Suddenly, Addy had an idea. She decided to stop by Mr. Delmonte's shop again on the way home, just to be sure the soft red scarf was still there. As she approached the store, Mr. Delmonte was just locking up.

"Don't worry, Addy," he said kindly. "The scarf is still here."

Mr. Delmonte headed down the street, but Addy lingered at the window for a moment. Then she headed back to Mrs. Ford's shop, thinking about her idea. *If I put half my tips in the milk bottle,* she thought, *and keep the other half, maybe I can save enough money to buy the scarf for Momma!*

By the time she got to the shop, her feet were numb with cold and her nose felt frozen.

"You look frozen stiff, child," said Mrs. Ford, peering above her spectacles. Mrs. Ford had a tape measure draped around her neck. Momma had a ribbon thrown across one shoulder as she sewed fringe on the end of a sash. They looked busy, and Addy knew she shouldn't bother them.

"Momma, can I light the stove upstairs now?" asked Addy. "Please?"

"No, Addy," Momma answered. "You know we don't light the stove until I start cooking supper. You head on upstairs. I'll be up as soon as I finish this sash."

"Yes, Momma," said Addy.

As she headed out the door, she heard Mrs. Ford ask Momma, "How is everything up in the garret?"

"Fine," Momma answered quickly. "We get by."

Addy wanted to turn around and tell Mrs. Ford the truth, that it was dark and freezing in the garret. She wanted to tell Mrs. Ford about the broken window and the snow on the floor. But Addy knew Momma would not want her to complain.

"We get by," Addy said softly to herself as she climbed the stairs.

When she got to the top, she lit the candle on the table. Addy turned her mitten upside down and let her tips fall onto the table. She brought the milk bottle out from behind the stove and set it next to the money. Then Addy went over to the bed and lifted up a corner of the mattress. There she found the kerchief that she had brought from the plantation when she and Momma had escaped from slavery. Tied in one corner was the half dime Uncle Solomon had given her. It was the only money they had when they headed north for freedom. *Freedom's got its cost,* Uncle Solomon had said when he gave it to Addy. She had saved it for something very special, something important.

Addy brought the kerchief over to the table and divided her tip money into two piles. She dropped one pile into the milk bottle and then carefully tied the other coins into the corner of her kerchief. With Uncle Solomon's half dime, she had ten cents in the kerchief. That was half of what she needed for Momma's red scarf. *I'm halfway there!* Addy thought to herself. The thought made her so happy that she didn't think about the cold.

THE COST OF FREEDOM
⌒ Chapter 13 ⌒

A t church the next morning, Momma and Addy sat side by side in the women's section. Addy looked across the aisle where all the men sat and imagined that someday her poppa would be sitting over there, smiling and giving her a wink that said, "You my favorite girl."

When the deep notes of the organ sounded, everyone stood to sing. The first song was one of Addy's favorites. Auntie Lula had taught it to her back on the plantation. Now Addy sang out with the others in joy.

> *This little light of mine,*
> *I'm gonna let it shine,*
> *Let it shine, let it shine, let it shine.*

After a long prayer, Reverend Drake began his sermon. "I want to begin this morning by reading from the Book of Luke. Turn to chapter two, verses six and seven. This passage is about Mary and Joseph."

Momma took a Bible from the rack on the pew in front of them. Addy helped her find the passage. They followed along as Reverend Drake read: "And she brought forth her firstborn son, and wrapped him in swaddling clothes, and laid him in a manger; because there was no room in the inn.

"Now, this is the story of Christmas, the story of the birth of Jesus. The time had come for Mary to give birth to Jesus. Let me tell you people, time is a curious thing. It can't be stopped like a clock," Reverend Drake said.

"You right, Reverend," one church member called out.

"Time keeps right on moving. And I'm here to tell you the *time* for freedom has come for thousands of our people. These freedmen are waiting right now in Washington, D.C., and other cities," Reverend Drake preached. "And they need our help, because freedom ain't free!"

A church member said, "You preaching the truth!"

Addy scooted closer to Momma and laid her head on Momma's shoulder. Momma put her arm around Addy and rocked gently on the pew. Addy liked coming to church. Anyone who wanted to could take part in the service. If you felt like answering the reverend, you could. If you felt like crying, or laughing, or clapping to the music the choir sang, you could.

Reverend Drake continued, "Some of you already know what I'm talking about because there was a *time* when you came to freedom, and you found out what freedom was about. It wasn't free! You needed food to eat, clothes to wear, a place to stay."

"Amen!" Momma replied.

"I'm here to tell you people, time ain't gonna stop for those thousands of freedmen who need our help. As I speak to you, babies are being born, and children are hungry, and mothers and fathers have no place to lay their heads at night. They need our help now, today!" Reverend Drake said, his voice getting louder.

Addy looked up at Momma and saw tears running down her face. Addy gave Momma a little hug.

"As we enter the season of Advent, the time of preparing for Christmas, let God work through you. When the collection boxes are passed this morning, remember to put in a little extra for our Freedmen's Fund. These people are your cousins, your brothers and sisters, your mothers and fathers," Reverend Drake said, pounding on the pulpit. "It might mean you have to sacrifice. If you can't give of your money, give of your time. Next Saturday a group of freedmen are coming in at the pier. Come help us welcome them to freedom.

On the way home from church, Momma and Addy walked hand in hand. Momma said, "I been thinking about what Reverend Drake said. He made me remember how it was for you and me when we first came to Philadelphia.

We had nothing. The church helped us when we needed it. Now we done saved more than a dollar fifty. The freedmen need our help right now. They need our savings more than we do. We can get along without a lamp, but they can't get along without help. What do you think?"

At first, Addy said nothing. It was true. She and Momma could get along without the lamp. But they had saved so hard for it. A lamp would help her see better when she did her homework, and it would help Momma when she had to sew late at night. But then Addy remembered how scared and lonely she and Momma had been when they first came to Philadelphia, and how the church had helped them find work, a place to live, and friends.

"I think we should give our money to the church," Addy said. "Other people helped us. The money might even help Sam or Poppa or Esther come to us."

"Even if it don't," replied Momma, "it's gonna help *somebody*. That's what's important." She squeezed Addy's hand. "We'll give the church our money next Sunday."

With a pang of guilt, Addy remembered the ten cents she had knotted up in her kerchief. Should she give that to help the freedmen, too? *No*, thought Addy. *I can't give that money away. It's for Momma's Christmas surprise.* Addy decided to keep the money. She was determined to buy the scarf and show Momma how much she loved her. She would find another way to help the freedmen.

Addy thought about what Reverend Drake had said about the group of freedmen arriving at the pier. "Momma," she asked, "can I go to the pier next Saturday to help out with the freedmen?"

"I think that would be fine, Addy," said Momma, "just so you finish all of Mrs. Ford's deliveries."

"I will, Momma," Addy promised.

When Addy arrived at the pier the next Saturday, Reverend Drake was already handing out clothes and blankets to the people who had just gotten off the boat. The newly freed people huddled together in silent groups. They looked cold, frightened, hungry, and lost. Addy closed her eyes for a second. *Esther. Sam. Poppa. Be here. Be here,* Addy wished. But when she opened her eyes, there were no familiar faces in the crowd.

Just then Addy saw a thin woman who held a bundle in her arms. Then she saw a little hand reach up from the bundle. Quickly, Addy pulled her shawl from around her shoulders and handed it to the woman, who thanked her and wrapped the shawl around her baby.

Addy held out her arms. "I can carry the baby, if you like," she said. "I'll be careful."

The woman smiled weakly and handed the baby to

Addy. "Thank you kindly," she said. Addy held the baby close to her chest, hoping to warm her. The baby waved her arms and grabbed the cowrie shell Addy wore around her neck. The woman smiled. "She like you," she said. "She don't take a shine to just anybody."

"Where y'all from?" Addy asked the baby's mother.

"We coming up from Baltimore," said the woman. "All the slaves on our plantation was turned out about a month ago. We was told we was free and we had to get. But we ain't had nowhere to go. No food. No nothing. Me and some others walked together. For a week, we ate almost nothing but grass. We walked until we got to Baltimore."

"Things gonna be better here," promised Addy. "The people at the church helped me and my momma. They'll help you, too."

When the group arrived back at church, Addy led the woman to Fellowship Hall in the basement. The big room was warm and dry and filled with the smell of delicious food. Many church members were there to help serve food to the freedmen. Addy remembered how happy she and Momma had been in this same place, eating their first meal in freedom on their first day in Philadelphia. She said good-bye to the woman. "You be safe now," she said. "People in the church gonna be your family." Addy hugged the baby one last time. Memories of Esther filled her mind, and she squeezed her eyes tight to stop the tears. Then Addy left to go to Mrs. Ford's.

Back at the shop, there were three deliveries to make. As Addy hurried along the busy streets, she saw women in fancy hats and fur coats. Usually Addy would have been fascinated with their fine clothes, but today she thought about the people shivering at the pier. When Addy made a delivery to one of the biggest houses on Society Hill, all she could think of were the freedmen who had arrived that morning. None of them had a place to stay at all.

Addy got tips from the first two houses she went to. The coins jingled in her mitten. If she got a five-cent tip from her last delivery, she would have enough for the scarf. Addy began to walk faster. Her last delivery was the beautiful plaid dress for Isabella Howell. It was the dress Momma had worked the hardest on, and Addy was very proud to be delivering it. She lifted the shiny brass knocker on the front door and banged it loudly three times.

Soon a woman came. "Who are you?" she asked coldly.

"I'm Addy Walker. This here is a dress from Mrs. Ford's dress shop. It's for Isabella Howell."

The maid took the package. "Wait here," she said.

Addy stood in the entrance of the Howells' mansion. The house was beautiful. A staircase of dark wood curved up to the second floor. Addy could see into the living room, too. She saw a high-backed pink couch and pink chairs. In the corner, a decorated Christmas tree reached up to the ceiling. Lamplight filled the room with a rosy glow, and a fire burned in the hearth.

The maid returned and pressed a coin into Addy's hand. "Here's a tip for you, child. Now run along," she said, hurrying Addy out the door.

The big door had closed behind her before Addy looked at the coin in her hand. She couldn't believe what she saw. "A dime!" said Addy out loud. "A whole dime." It was the biggest tip Addy had ever gotten. Now she had enough for Momma's scarf!

Addy slid the dime into her mitten and ran all the way back to the shop. She ran upstairs, took her kerchief out from under the mattress, and let the coins fall on the table. She turned her mitten upside down and dumped the tips she had made that day into the pile of money. She counted twenty cents for Momma's scarf. Then she dropped the rest of the money in the milk bottle. The twenty cents went into her mitten. She would get the scarf this afternoon after she finished her errands. She could hardly wait!

Addy's last chore of the day was to get Mrs. Ford's scissors sharpened. The sharpener's shop was not too far from Mr. Delmonte's shop. If Addy hurried, she could get the scissors sharpened and buy the scarf before it got dark.

The grinding wheel that sharpened the scissors made a loud whining noise, so Addy waited outside. Streetcars clanged and carriages rushed by, but she hardly noticed them. All she could think about was Momma's scarf and how surprised she would be on Christmas morning.

A woman pushing a fancy baby buggy wheeled toward Addy. The baby started to fuss, and Addy remembered the baby she'd held that morning. Then she began to think about Esther. *My sister might not be as lucky as that baby at the pier. Who's gonna give money for her to come to freedom?*

Addy felt the coins she held inside her mitten. It was only twenty cents. But if everyone gave as much as possible, then all the newly freed people could get to the North— maybe even Esther. As Addy went back inside the shop to pick up the scissors, her heart ached with the memory of her baby sister.

Addy headed toward Mr. Delmonte's store. It was still open. She could see the pretty red scarf tucked behind the teakettle in the window. But Addy didn't go inside. Instead, she walked on down the street for a few more blocks until she came to the church. With both hands, she pulled open the heavy door. She walked over to the box at the side of the church. Above it was a sign that said "Freedmen's

Fund." Slowly, Addy took off her mitten. One by one, she dropped her coins into the box. The last coin was the half dime Uncle Solomon had given her. She remembered the words he said to her, *Freedom's got its cost.* Then she thought of Esther, Sam, and Poppa, still waiting to take their freedom, and she let the half dime clink into the box with the rest of her money.

When Addy got back to the shop, Momma and Mrs. Ford looked up when Addy came through the door.

"There won't be any more deliveries today," said Mrs. Ford.

As Addy turned to leave, Mrs. Ford said, "There's no sense in you going upstairs. Stay here with me and your mother."

Addy could not believe her ears! Did Mrs. Ford say she could stay in the shop?

Momma said, "Addy will be all right upstairs, Mrs. Ford. I know you running a business here, and you don't want children in the shop."

"I know I've said that in the past," Mrs. Ford said to Momma, "but I believe that Addy has served my business well, and I don't think she'll be in the way."

As Addy removed her coat and hat, Mrs. Ford handed her a needle and thread. "You can keep yourself busy. I know your mother's taught you how to make a hem. Here is a plain apron you can practice on."

"Oh, thank you, Mrs. Ford," Addy said.

"There's no need to thank me," Mrs. Ford said as she went back to her sewing.

"Come sit on this crate by me," Momma said. "I'll keep an eye on your stitches."

Addy sat down next to Momma and spread the white apron across her lap. She threaded the needle and knotted it tight. She picked up the corner of the apron and started to sew the hem. Carefully and slowly, Addy went about her task. She concentrated hard on her stitches, making them even and straight.

Addy was glad to have a job to do. It helped take her mind off the scarf. But more than anything, she was glad to be with Momma.

CHRISTMAS SURPRISES
⁀ Chapter 14 ⁀

rom that day on, Addy was allowed to spend afternoons sewing in the warm shop with Momma and Mrs. Ford instead of in the cold garret by herself. Business had begun to slow down. Momma and Mrs. Ford were just finishing up a few small items.

Four days before Christmas, Addy was straightening up the shop when the door burst open. An angry woman stormed in, and a tall, plump girl followed. Addy knew the woman must be Mrs. Howell because she carried the beautiful green plaid dress that Momma had worked so hard on. The woman thrust the dress toward Mrs. Ford.

"Look at this dress," Mrs. Howell fumed. "Just look at it!" The seams on the sides were split open, and the threads of the plaid fabric were frayed. The buttons on the back had popped off.

"This dress was made too small," Mrs. Howell raged. "I've never seen such poor work."

Addy looked at Momma, who kept her eyes on the sewing in her lap while her lips tightened in anger.

"Stop right there," Mrs. Ford said firmly. "Ruth Walker

here is the best seamstress I've ever had working for me.
I am sure the dress was sewn to the exact measurements we
took at the fitting last month. Perhaps Isabella has grown."

Addy looked at Isabella. She stood near the door, looking at her feet. Her round face flushed pink.

Mrs. Ford went on. "If you are unhappy, I will give
you a full refund, Mrs. Howell—not because the dress was
poorly made, but because you are dissatisfied."

Mrs. Ford gave Mrs. Howell a handful of bills. "Now
good day to you, madam," Mrs. Ford said coldly.

"Good day!" said Mrs. Howell. A blast of cold air blew
into the shop as the door slammed behind them.

Mrs. Ford sat back down. As she picked up her sewing,
she said, "I can't believe she acted that way. Some people
have no idea what the Christmas season is all about."

Addy made her last delivery on the day before Christmas. When she returned to the shop in the early afternoon,
Momma wasn't there.

"She's gone upstairs for a rest," Mrs. Ford explained.
"Your mother's worked hard."

Addy started to head up to the garret, but Mrs. Ford
stopped her. "There's one last package." She handed a
parcel wrapped in brown paper to Addy. "Open it. It's
for you."

Addy untied the package and could hardly believe what was inside. It was the green plaid dress Momma had made for Isabella Howell! But it looked like new. All the seams were repaired and the buttons had been replaced.

"I want you to have this dress, Addy," Mrs. Ford said. "You've been such a big help to your mother and me."

Addy didn't know what to say.

"I've made the dress smaller to fit you," Mrs. Ford went on. "The hem just needs to be cut to the right length. Slip the dress on and I'll pin it up before I leave."

"Yes, ma'am," Addy said.

Addy stood on a crate while Mrs. Ford knelt on the floor, measuring the hem. Addy turned in a circle, taking tiny steps as the skirt of the dress was pinned to the proper length. Then she took off the dress so Mrs. Ford could cut off the extra material.

When Mrs. Ford was finished, the long, wide piece of material she had cut from the bottom of the dress was hanging around her neck. Seeing it gave Addy an idea.

"Mrs. Ford, can I have the material you cut from the dress?" asked Addy.

"Certainly," replied Mrs. Ford. "I'll be leaving now, but you can stay down here where the light is better and sew up the hem. When you're through, don't forget to put out the lamp."

"Yes, ma'am," said Addy. "And thank you, Mrs. Ford."

"You're welcome, Addy," said Mrs. Ford. "Merry Christmas."

::

On Christmas morning, Addy and Momma woke early, Momma spoke first. "I know you awake, Addy. Merry Christmas."

"Merry Christmas, Momma," Addy said, sitting up in bed. Sunlight streamed through the frosty windowpanes, which looked as though they were covered with a delicate lace.

"I got a surprise for you, honey," said Momma. She handed Addy a small parcel wrapped in paper.

Addy untied the string. As the paper fell away, she saw a rag doll with a bright red smile stitched on her face. She had a bow tucked in her hair and tiny hoop earrings.

Addy hugged the doll. "She so pretty."

Momma beamed. "I stuffed her with some beans I saved."

"Then I'll call her Ida Bean," said Addy with a giggle. "Now I got a surprise for you, too, Momma. Hide your eyes because it ain't wrapped." Addy hopped out of bed and picked up her school satchel. She took out the gift she'd hidden inside. Then she placed her gift on Momma's lap.

"Now you can open your eyes," said Addy.

When Momma looked down, there was a lovely scarf of beautiful green plaid before her. The edges were sewn with tiny perfect stitches and the ends were fringed.

"Where'd you get this?" asked Momma in surprise.

Addy told Momma all about the dress Mrs. Ford had repaired for her and about the extra material that was left when she cut off the bottom to make the dress fit Addy. "I made the extra material into a scarf for you, Momma," Addy explained.

"Oh, Addy," said Momma gently, running her hands across the plaid. "It's beautiful. Ain't we gonna look fine going to church this evening?" Momma gave Addy a long hug. "I'm proud of my girl!" she said.

After breakfast, Addy propped Ida Bean in a chair so she could watch as Addy and Momma made sweet-potato pudding. There was some pudding left over, so Momma put it in a small pan.

"We can leave this one here and have it tomorrow," Momma said.

When it was time to get ready for church, Addy put on her beautiful new dress, and Momma took time braiding Addy's hair. Momma put her new scarf around her neck and tied it in a big bow. Then they headed out to church.

Addy and Momma had just been seated when a loud chord blasted from the organ. The choir began to walk down the aisle singing "Joy to the World" in strong, happy voices. A glow filled the dark church as the choir marched in. Each member held a candle that cast shadows into the church. Sarah, who was at the front of the choir, smiled at Addy. Addy gave a shy wave back.

When the service was over, everyone went down to Fellowship Hall for dinner. There was turkey and dressing, squash and greens, corn bread and applesauce. When it was time to go back for dessert, Addy ignored all the cakes and pies and headed straight for Momma's sweet-potato pudding. As she savored each bite, she thought about Poppa, Sam, and Esther. *Maybe next Christmas, we'll all be together, eating Momma's sweet-potato pudding.*

After dinner, the children hurried to the room set up for the shadow play. Sarah and Addy sat on a bench next to each other. When all the children were settled, the door was closed, the lamps on the walls were blown out, and the room was completely dark. After a minute, a lamp began to glow behind the sheet in the front of the room. All eyes watched as the first shadow figure appeared on the sheet and the Christmas story was read aloud.

One figure and then another and another appeared on the sheet until soon Addy could see the shadow of Mary bent over the manger, holding her newborn baby, with Joseph standing at her side. A deep, rolling voice continued to read as all the children sat in the dark, quietly watching the shapes against the lighted sheet.

As the star appeared to guide the wise men, the door at the side of the room opened. A shaft of light from the hall filled the darkened room. The children turned to see who had opened the door. It was a tall man. Though Addy could not see his face, his silhouette was a shape she recognized. Addy jumped up and struggled past the girl next to her, tripping over her feet, stumbling as she hurried to the door. Addy knew who was standing in the door, standing

there right now, not someday, but right now.

"Poppa," she burst out. "Poppa, is that you?"

"Is that my Addy?" came the answer.

It was Poppa! Addy rushed to him, and he swept her up into his strong arms and held her close for a long time.

::

It was dark by the time Addy, Poppa, and Momma headed back to the garret, walking hand in hand through the Christmas streets. When they got to the top of the stairs above Mrs. Ford's shop, Addy could see light under their door.

"That's strange," Momma said. "We didn't leave the candle burning."

When they opened the door, there on the table was a kerosene lamp shining brightly. Addy picked up the note

lying beside it and read it out loud. "May the hope of the Christmas season shine in your lives always. Merry Christmas from Mrs. Ford," she read.

Addy looked at Poppa. He was crying. "What's wrong, Poppa?" she asked.

Poppa sat down in a chair. "I'm crying because I'm so happy. I'm so proud you can read," he said. "I always knew you was a smart girl."

"Addy doing so good in school," Momma said.

"She won a prize for spelling."

"Momma can read, too. And write," said Addy. "I been helping her, and I can help you."

Addy picked up Ida Bean and crawled into Poppa's lap. Momma and Addy told Poppa about leaving Esther with Auntie Lula and Uncle Solomon and escaping into the woods and on to freedom in Philadelphia.

Then Poppa told Addy and Momma about the time since he was taken from them.

"Me and Sam was separated that very next day. I don't know where they took him."

"Maybe he escaped," Addy said hopefully.

"Maybe," Poppa said. "If there was a way for your brother to run, I know he found it. I couldn't, though. I was bound hand and foot all the way to my new plantation. And after all that, all us slaves on the plantation was freed two months after I got there."

"How you find your way here?" Addy asked.

"There was a freedmen's society in Maryland that helped me," Poppa explained. "Maybe the freedmen's society in Philadelphia can help us get Esther and Sam back so we all can be together in freedom like we planned."

Addy laid her head against Poppa's chest. She felt certain that their dream would happen.

"It's time you got ready for bed, Addy," Momma said.

"Can't I stay up longer?" Addy asked.

"You gonna sit up all night like an owl?" Poppa teased.

Addy laughed. "I want to stay up and be with you."

"Well, I ain't going nowhere. I'm gonna be here when you wake up in the morning," Poppa said. "I'll be the first thing you see when the sun comes in that window."

"That window got stuck about a month ago and we can't get it down," Momma said.

"Let me have a look at it," Poppa said. He lifted Addy off his lap and they all went over to the window. Poppa studied the window and then hit the frame in two places. Then he pulled down hard and closed the window.

"There!" said Poppa. "It needs a new sash. I can make that. But it should be warmer in here now."

"It already is," said Addy. She and Momma put their arms around Poppa. In the window, Addy could see their happy faces reflected in the glow of the lamplight.

INSIDE
ADDY'S WORLD

More than 300 years before Addy was born, the first black people arrived in America on slave ships. Slave traders had captured or bought them in Africa, taking them from their families, their tribes, and their homeland. In Africa they had a life rich in art, religion, music, and language. But in America they were forced to work against their will, without pay, for life.

By Addy's time, most enslaved people worked on *plantations*, or large farms, in the southern United States. Plantation owners in the South depended on slaves to tend their crops because that was a cheap way to get the work done. Most plantation slaves were field hands who planted,

The man on horseback is buying slaves who have just arrived on a ship from Africa. The dome of the U.S. Capitol, with an American flag, is in the background.

Field slaves at work on a cotton plantation

tended, and harvested crops, but some slaves were blacksmiths, shoe-makers, and carpenters, like Addy's father, or worked in their owners' houses as cooks, nursemaids, and seamstresses, like Addy's mother.

The treatment of slaves varied widely, but owners usually provided just enough food and clothing for slaves to survive. Most slaves lived in one-room cabins with dirt floors. Owners might punish them by whipping them, shackling their feet and hands, or making them eat tobacco worms, as Addy had to. Worst of all, owners could sell slaves and divide families, as Addy's owner did.

By the early 1800s, most northern states had made slavery illegal. And in 1808, it became illegal to bring slaves into the United States. But the buying and selling of slaves continued in the South until Addy's time.

Slaves were considered property. When an own sold a slave, he separate family members forever

People who were against slavery were called *abolitionists.* Abolitionists, both black and white, helped slaves escape on the Underground Railroad, a series of routes and hiding "stations" leading north to freedom. Escaping slaves trav-eled at night, hidden by darkness, usually to the northern

Harriet Tubman escaped slavery and helped over 300 runaway slaves gain freedom.

states or Canada. Harriet Tubman, an escaped slave herself, secretly returned to the South nineteen times to guide others to freedom. Escaping required great courage, because runaway slaves who were caught were brutally punished.

When Addy and her mother escaped, northern states were fighting against southern states in the Civil War. This war had many causes, but one of the most important was the disagreement about slavery. People in the North felt slavery should not be legal. In 1861, several southern states *seceded*, or separated, from the United States. These states formed their own nation, called the Confederate States of America. President Abraham Lincoln believed it was wrong for the southern states to secede, and he eventually declared war against the South. That war was called the War Between the States, or the Civil War.

On January 1, 1863, Lincoln proclaimed that all slaves in states still fighting the North were *emancipated*, or free. Because the South had decided that it was a separate nation, it ignored the Emancipation Proclamation. That's why many people, like Addy's family, were still risking their lives to escape slavery in 1864.

Eleven southern states left the Union to form the Confederate States of America.

It was against the law in most southern states to teach African Americans to read and write. Many white people did not want black people to be able to read about freedom in the North because they were afraid their slaves would run away. They also didn't want them to write for fear that they would write notes called *passes* that said they were free to leave the plantation.

Even in the North, where there was no slavery, black students were usually taught in separate schools from white students, as Addy was in Philadelphia. This separation is called *segregation*. Schools for black children had fewer supplies, and the buildings were poorly maintained compared with those for white children.

During the Civil War, many slaves ran away to freedom

or were set free by Union troops from the North. These newly freed slaves were called *freedmen*. Churches and other groups in the North began to send teachers to teach the freedmen. African American adults and children flocked to these schools in the South, though they often faced anger and even threats to their lives from white people who wanted black people to stay uneducated and enslaved. Freedmen often took great risks to get an education.

By the time Addy was in school, thousands of black people had learned to read and write. They knew that education meant true freedom—that education opened the door to better jobs and better lives.

A school for freed slaves during the Civil War

A HEART FULL OF HOPE

Addy's hands trembled. *Please let this letter be good news,* she prayed. She took a deep breath and began to read:

> I am writing to inform you that Solomon and Lula Morgan came to a freedman's camp where I've been working. They had a baby girl with them. They were heading to Philadelphia —

Addy stopped reading. "They got to be in Philadelphia by now! Maybe they're here but ain't found us yet."

"Uncle Solomon and Auntie Lula real old," Poppa said. "They can't travel fast. They could've run into bad weather or had to stop at another camp on the way."

"We got to start looking for them," Addy said.

"Yes, we do," said Momma. "We can keep searching the aid societies and the churches . . ."

"We been working together as a family, and that's what we gonna keep on doing," Poppa said.

"And together we gonna find Esther and Auntie Lula and Uncle Solomon and bring them home!" Addy said confidently.

Later that night, when Addy was in bed, she looked over at Momma, whose head was bent over her sewing. Addy loved to watch Momma sew different-shaped pieces of cloth together so that they fit together perfectly. When Momma sewed, it was as if she were working on a puzzle that always came out right. There was never a missing piece. Addy hoped her family would soon be joined together like that, whole and safe.

"Who you making the dress for?" Addy asked.

Momma looked up and smiled. "Esther," she said. "I picked out this here fabric a while back, but I ain't dare start nothing for Esther. It didn't seem right. But now I think Esther gonna be with us soon."

Addy closed her eyes and said an extra special prayer for Esther and Auntie Lula and Uncle Solomon. *Tomorrow*, Addy thought, *we gonna start looking for you in Philadelphia.*

a Nez Perce girl who
loves daring adventures
on horseback

a Hispanic girl
growing up on a rancho
in New Mexico

who is determined
to be free in the midst
of the Civil War

a Jewish girl with
a secret ambition to
be an actress

who faces the
Great Depression with
determination and grit

who joins the
war effort when Hawaii
is attacked

whose big ideas get
her into trouble—but
also save the day

who finds the
strength to lift her voice
for those who can't

who fights for the
right to play on the
boys' basketball team